A Collection

OF MADNESS

Tristan Duerr

Acknowledgments

Developmental editing by Leanne Felton

Further editing by Robin Cain

Formatting by Tina Holland

Special thanks to the Moorhead Friends Writing Group for being inspirations to all.

And lastly, you the reader, for helping make my dreams come true.

DEDICATION

For my friends and family.
Who gave me support when I thought I had none.

Contents

THE WENDIGO

I sat in my small apartment, bored as all hell. I had no plans, and no idea what I'd do with my day. Outside my bedroom window were the busy, bustling streets of the city, and they were filled with people of all kinds: people going to work, waiting for buses, and sitting on outdoor chairs at restaurants, just like I'd seen every day.

City life was nice and all, as there was unlimited access to pretty much anything I could ever want. A coffee shop across the street at which to relax, underground metros that could take me anywhere, and restaurants as far as the eye could see. But I'd be lying if I didn't admit that it got boring after a while, seeing the same buildings and scenery day in and day out. A tall grey building was followed by another then another, stretching on like metallic vines that had grown too long. Then there were the mundane routines. Wake up, make noodles, go to work, relax at a coffee shop, get something to eat, go home, rest, sleep then do it all again. It drained me and I started to get the feeling of being trapped and insanely bored as I constantly felt like I was just going through the motions and living life without truly living.

I remembered the days of being a child and living in the countryside before I left for college. I had many adventures in the woods behind my house, playing and pretending that I was a hero inside of a woodland realm, climbing the trees like Tarzan, or building little forts that felt like castles. I longed for something like that again one day. I decided that I would stop sitting around wishing for adventure and just do it. It was summer and I didn't have to worry about classes, so I decided to take a week off of work to spend plenty of time out there. I then got the idea to bring some friends along to add to the fun. I took out my phone and called my friend Sam.

"Hello?" A deep voice said from the other end.

I could hardly contain my excitement when I heard his voice on the other end. "Hey Sam, it's Eric."

"Oh hey, man," Sam said in an excited tone. We hadn't talked at all in the past week due to both of us being swamped with work, so it was nice to hear that he was just as excited to talk as I was.

"Are you doing anything at all next week," I asked him, hoping with all my heart that he would give me the answer I desired.

"My schedule is clear. Why?" He seemed even more excited now.

"I've been cooped up in my apartment for too long and thought about getting the group together for a camping trip."

Before I could even ask if he was interested, he shouted, "Yes!"

"Alright then, I was thinking we could leave Monday and spend the whole week there. I'll start planning things out if you want to let the others know." He agreed and in doing so he unknowingly inched ever closer to his oblivion.

I immediately packed my bags. I filled them with all one would need for a trip: water, food, games, a tent, and so on. When the day came, we decided to meet at a local grocery store in case anyone needed to grab any last-minute items. When I arrived, Sam was already there, leaning against his car. He was a bit of a workout nut, to say the least. Broad shoulders, large biceps, and legs that could squat over 400 pounds. He wasn't some typical jock though. He was a kind and approachable guy who simply liked to work out.

"Hey Sam, I had a feeling you'd be the first one here,"

"Of course, I wouldn't miss this for the world, especially since everyone else is coming," he said in an upbeat tone, his leg jittering slightly.

"I know how you feel. I was glad everyone else could make it too," I said. "Speaking of which, has anyone else arrived yet?"

"Gabe's in the store grabbing a few last-minute things before everyone else gets here." As Sam said this, the city bus stopped by the edge of the parking lot. I smiled as another of our friends, Odisia, stepped out.

"Hey guys, did I keep you waiting?" she asked as she walked over to us. A sense of calm washed over me when I heard her voice. To say it was good to see her again was an understatement.

"Not at all. It's Gabe currently making us wait," I said.

"He's been in there for ages," Sam said, rolling his eyes. "He said he'd be quick but it's been an hour now."

"An hour? What could he be grabbing," Odisia asked.

"I have no idea," Sam said with a sigh. "If my car didn't have functioning air conditioning, I would've left him by now," Sam said with a chuckle. He was too kind for that, but it was ninety degrees outside so I don't think I could find it in my heart to forgive him if he did.

As we waited Odisia walked over to me and asked, "So what's new?"

"Nothing much honestly. Been swamped with work and assignments so I haven't had much free time."

"I know what you mean," she said, letting out a sigh. It felt nice to chat with her again. My work had affected my personal life, so my time with friends had been affected. The routine was sheer boredom. I was surviving in the sense that work gave me money to live, and the school gave me something to work towards, but it wasn't living. Being around genuine friends again seemed to take a weight off my shoulders. I was no longer around people simply shuffling around from one class to the next because they paid thousands of dollars to be there, and it was a relief. But out of everyone I missed, I missed Odisia the most. While it was hard not being able to interact with everyone, it was especially hard with Odisia because I had a massive crush on her. I had been meaning to ask her out for a while but never found the right time. In all honesty, I suspected she may have a crush on me too, but that might have just been overconfidence kicking in.

"Well, we have time now, let's not waste it," I said as she shared a smile with me. She was about to say something in response but Gabe finally walked out of the store with several bags of supplies.

"Gabe, what's all this you said about only needing a few things," Sam asked, rolling his eyes again.

"Yeah, these are my essentials."

I looked through his bags and, judging by their contents, I could tell that he had pre-packed nothing. A particular item caught my eye. "Ah yes, vanilla rum, very essential indeed," I said.

"You're just mad you've got shit taste," Gabe said with all the bravado of Hugh Hefner.

We packed our clothes, food, water, and all the other necessities before piling into my truck and setting out. I rolled down the window to let in a cool breeze. The sun glowed warmly in the clear, blue sky. It was a time of blissful relaxation as the radio played music quietly. I had that special feeling you get when you're simply enjoying a good mood, the kind where you could tell you were in a moment you'd refer to as "the good days" later in life. The simple company was my vaccine to the virus of routine.

Gabe began to crack jokes and funny stories of past events. Even though he could get annoying at times, Gabe knew how to make people laugh.

"Do you guys remember when I swapped out Sam's protein drink with spoiled milk?"

We couldn't help but laugh a little, including Sam as he lightly punched Gabe on the shoulder.

"I was throwing up for ten minutes," Sam said.

Even though laughed about it, at the time, Sam wanted to kick Gabe's ass when he'd finished throwing up. But hey, events like that always made for good stories later in life, right? Luckily, Sam wasn't one to hold a grudge and had learned to tolerate Gabe's jokes.

"How old are you guys?" Odisia asked, laughing. I loved her laugh and her smile. There was so much joy behind them and seeing her that happy made her hard not to love. Seeing her and the rest of my friends happy and laughing brought back good times, memories: ones of us cheating off each other's tests in school, Sam beating our school's deadlift record, and how he'd cried because his win had made all of us so happy, to simply remembering those calm days when we just hung out. After all, we enjoyed each other's company. I'd give anything to have moments like those again.

We arrived at the same woods where I grew up. They felt like I was back home. The birds were singing and the wind was blowing through the trees. That was the last time those woods ever made me feel at peace.

We spent the rest of that day unpacking and setting up the campsite.

"Alright everyone," Sam called out. "Gabe and I will finish unpacking and setting up the fire pit while Eric and Odisia set up the tent. Sound good?"

We all agreed and got to work on our tasks. Odisha held the stakes in place while I hammered them into the ground.

"Thank you for inviting me," Odisha said. "I've missed hanging out with everyone."

"Yeah, of course, I wouldn't invite everyone else and then leave you out." I finished pushing in one of the stakes and moved to the next one. *Ting, ting, ting.* I gazed around, making sure Gabe and Sam were out of earshot. Once I made sure they couldn't hear me I said, "If I'm being honest, you were the one I most hoped would come."

Odisia seemed taken aback by this. "Why's that?" she asked.

"Well, you're the one I've seen the least since we graduated."

"That's partially my fault."

"We've both been busy so don't blame yourself. But other than that, you're a nice change of pace."

"What do you mean?"

"Don't get me wrong, I love talking with Sam and Gabe, but their interests and attitudes can get a bit much at times. You, on the other hand, bring a sense of calm whenever I speak to you."

She seemed stunned by this but then she smiled. "I missed you the most too."

We finished setting up the tent just in time to settle in for the night. We were all tired after setting up camp so we all decided to go to bed a bit early. I drifted off quickly, falling asleep to the soothing sounds of nature. That was until I heard a distant screech. I sat up and listened. After a few seconds, the sound drifted to my ears again. Whatever was making the noise was far away. When I heard it a third time I sighed. "It's just an elk." I laid back down and drifted off to sleep once again.

When I woke up early the following day I let out a big yawn. It was a wonderful morning. The sun shimmered, casting golden streaks through the clouds. I decided to explore the area around our camp and see if there were any important landmarks or anything of general interest. I found Sam (the only other one awake at the time) unpacking a clean set of clothes for himself.

"I'm gonna have a look around. Let everyone else know where I am if they wake up."

Sam nodded. "Don't get lost."

I walked for about ten minutes or so when I started to smell something horrid. It smelled like my grandfather's garage when he skinned the animals he had hunted. I followed the smell out of both curiosity and concern. If it really was a dead animal, I wanted to know what had killed it. If it was natural causes then it would be fine. If it was clear it had been attacked then we may have to worry about predators in the area. After following the smell, I soon discovered it was a deer.

I could hardly tell by looking at it though. It was mangled. Large bites and slashes covered its body. Blood covered the surrounding plant life and the corpse had been stripped of most of its skin and organs. I fell back, startled by the sight of the corpse. I'd seen dead animals before, even ones that had been eaten. Even when my grandfather skinned them there was a process, a clean way of doing it, but this was savagery. I quickly ran back to camp to tell everyone about what I had seen. Everyone was awake and looked at me confused when I came bursting through the bushes.

"There you are," Gabe said. "Are you okay? You look panicked."

I placed my hands on my knees as I panted heavily. I then waved one hand, "I'm okay." I caught my breath and said, "I saw a dead deer in the woods."

"You had me worried for a second," Sam said. "We're in the wilderness, so it's not exactly random to see a dead animal."

"Normally I'd agree with you, but this deer had been completely ripped apart."

"Do you think it could've been a bear?" Odissia asked.

"Maybe, but this seemed way too savage. Regardless of what it was, I think we should move our camp away from this area," I said.

Gabe sighed. "But we just got all setup," Gabe said. "Now we have to do it all over again?"

"Would you rather set up camp again, or wonder what's gonna be in our camp while we sleep?" Sam said to Gabe.

"I'm sure we could take whatever it is," Gabe said confidently.

"Will you be so naive if it's a grizzly bear?" Odisia said, giving him a look of annoyance.

Gabe tried to get a comeback in, but not wanting to see my friends argue when we were supposed to be having fun, I said, "Guys, guys, I know we're tired but we don't need to argue over this. We'll quickly pack up, drive just a few more miles down the road to put some distance between us and the smell of the deer, and then we'll be good. I'll even put up your tent for you, Gabe." I said, hoping it would give him some incentive.

He sighed but agreed. "Can you carry me away from the monster to Prince Charming?" Gabe said and fluttered his eyes.

"No, we'll be able to escape faster if I'm not carrying you while we're being chased."

We quickly got all our gear packed and moved ourselves to our new location. On the way through the thick woods, I kept feeling like something was moving around the woods nearby. I'd hear small twig snaps or weird sounds that sounded far off. No one said anything so I thought I was just being paranoid. After we got a good distance away from the deer corpse, we set up our new camp. To treat ourselves, we decided to make some s'mores.

I took out my box of matches and got the fire started while Odisia got the ingredients out of the pack. The s'mores made me feel much better. The soft, sweet taste melted my worries away. Combined with the company of good friends, I nearly forgot about the deer.

Later that day, we walked to a nearby river and went fishing. I was surprised when I caught something within the first few minutes. In all the excitement, I almost missed Sam dashing towards Gabe and shoving him into the river. Gabe's fishing rod went flying out of his hands when he landed in the water. He thrashed around, attempting to get himself up while also trying to knock away whatever or whoever pushed him in. When he was able to fully stand and get the water out of his eyes, Sam stood there laughing at him.

"What was that for?" Gabe asked angrily, flipping back his wet hair.

"Payback for the milk," Sam said but he extended a hand.

Gabe's expression went from annoyed to prideful as Sam helped him out of the water. "Huh? I didn't think you had a sense of humor."

"I have my moments," Sam said, patting Gabe on the back.

After our fishing trip, we headed back to the camp. What we caught that day was our dinner.

"You know, I think our hunter-gatherer ancestors were onto something," Gabe said as we feasted on our catch. The rest of the meal was quiet but then I started to hear strange sounds again. The trees began to groan and creak louder, the fire crackled more intensely, and twigs seemed to snap harder. A black shadow moved across the bushes. It appeared to move through the shadows the fire caused.

"Eric, are you okay?" Odisha asked.

"I thought I saw something," I looked around and everything looked and sounded normal again. "Just shadows."

An hour later I decided to turn in for the night. Between having to move the camp and the fishing trip, I was tired. Kneeling to open my tent, I saw a long dark hand out of the corner of my eye. It was resting on a tree but quickly vanished when I looked in its direction. I drew my hunting knife and quietly walked over there. It was no longer there, but my heart pounded and my brain was screaming.

As I drew closer, my lungs felt like they had the air ripped from them. It was as if some primal instinct was pushing all my energy to the muscles in my body. My brain screamed, 'the tree, the tree. The monster is behind the tree.' I gritted my teeth and quickly moved to the side to see what monster was awaiting me, but to my shock, there was nothing there.

I took a deep breath and went back to the camp, deciding that the dead deer had made me more paranoid than I thought. Everyone had begun to clean up and turn in for the night. The sun slowly set, painting the sky with wondrous colors. My earlier fear was replaced with a sense of childlike wonder. This wonder made my heart flutter in the same way a lover's embrace would. Even with the day's horrors, I went into my tent that night with a smile on my face. About ten minutes passed before my body finally let me sleep then I heard my tent slowly open. I quickly sat up.

"Sorry if I startled you," Odisia whispered. "I didn't feel like sleeping yet."

"Don't worry about it. You can hang out here if you want."

We continued to talk, reflecting on all of the good and bad times that we'd been through together. At one point, we nestled closer together, closed our eyes, and kissed each other softly.

"Thank you," she said.

"For what?"

"For finally pulling the trigger," she said with a giggle. A noise outside the tent made us both turn our heads.

"Did you hear that?" I asked.

She nodded and a few seconds later I heard the sound of footsteps getting closer and closer.

"Is that Gabe?" I asked.

"He went to the bathroom when you went into your tent," Odisia whispered. That made me nervous. Why would Gabe take that long?

"It's me guys," Gabe said, allowing both of us to let out a sigh of relief, but then Sam screamed from a distance, followed by a second ear-splitting scream that nearly deafened me. It sounded like the elk's scream from earlier, but the scream was much clearer now. A shiver crawled up my spine with chilling fingers when I realized that this was the same sound. I quickly opened the tent. A tall, lanky humanoid-looking creature was tearing into Sam's tent. The creature's skin was nearly as dark as the night sky and was pulled so tightly that I could see a perfect outline of the creature's bones as if it had been starved for weeks.

My mind raced. How could such a monstrous thing possibly exist? The tent was nearly torn to shreds. Fabric and bent metal rods from inside the tent littered the ground. The beast had torn it up so completely that Sam could be seen struggling underneath it as the creature attempted to sink its claws into him. Just as the creature ripped away the last scrap of the tent from Sam, it suddenly let out another ear-splitting roar. Sam stabbed the creature with a large knife, which made the creature stumble back in pain. Sam quickly got out of the tent's remains and simply shouted at us. "Run!"

The three of us ran as the creature roared out in pain, its shriek deafening. This horrid shriek pierced through my ears like an icepick. That's when it hit me. What I heard on our first night wasn't an elk. It was this thing. It had been following us ever since we arrived.

Sam was cradling his arm that the creature had scratched when it was trying to get to him. Luckily it didn't seem that bad. He could still move it so it hadn't sliced the tendon. We ran until our lungs burned then hid behind a fallen tree.

"Where the fuck is Gabe?" I whispered

"I have no idea. He never came back from the bathroom," Sam said.

"Then who came back just before you were attacked?" Odisia asked.

"It was that thing, speaking in Gabe's voice."

That statement sent a shiver down my spine, but the sound of footsteps made my heart stop.

The creature, using Gabe's voice, called out, "Guys, where are you?" The footsteps stopped. We were surrounded by an eerie quiet, though the quiet didn't last long before being broken by a crackled, distorted voice from the depths of hell.

"I CAN SMELL YOU."

Suddenly, the creature's long, black hand slammed down on the top of the log with such force that it imprinted a distorted handprint on the wood. Despite our horror, Sam somehow managed to act quickly and stab the hand of the creature. The creature roared again and then threw the log like it was a paperweight. I could then see the creature's nightmarish face. It had the head of a deer but no skin.

The creature let out another roar but this time in a crackling version of Gabe's voice, as if it had come through T.V. static. Sam threw himself at the creature and began to plunge his knife into the creature over and over again, going for its stomach and ribs. Red, thick blood coated them both as he drove the knife into its tight flesh. The flesh, which had been pulled so tightly, was now released, and its skin now hung along its bones. Despite the damage, the creature didn't slow, its rage didn't subside, and its hunger remained plentiful. The creature whipped its claws into Sam's body, letting out another noise. Not a roar of pain or rage, but a cackle of amusement. Crimson blood dripped down its long fingers.

"Get the fuck out of here," Sam said, his blood filling his throat and mouth.

Instinct taking over at that point, I grabbed Odisia's hand and ran as fast as our legs could carry.

All the memories I had of Sam rushed through my head: him defending me from bullies in middle school, helping me train to get stronger, and helping me move stuff into my apartment in the city. I'd live through a thousand lifetimes of my boring mundane routine and never go to the country again if it meant I could have kept my friend alive.

We got to the car, and I quickly retrieved the key from the rearview mirror. I jammed it into the ignition and pressed down on the gas pedal so hard I was astonished it didn't break. We raced down the road faster than I had ever driven before. Every evolutionary instinct told me to run.

"What the fuck was that?" Odisia said. She was as pale as a ghost. Her eyes were as wide as a full moon and her lungs heaved in the air as if she hadn't been breathing throughout the whole experience. Sneaking a glance at myself in the rearview mirror, I realized I looked even worse.

"I have no idea. Just let me--"

Something big slammed into the car. We flipped and crashed into the ditch next to the road. I blacked out for a few seconds but screams pulled me back into semi-consciousness. I woke up slowly. My vision was blurred, but I saw the creature standing above the car. It ripped off the car door like it was a piece of paper, then it grabbed Odisia. She screamed and cried and tried to hit the creature to get it to let go of her. But it was pointless. The creature jabbed its giant claws into her stomach and then ripped them out, opening up her body. Blood poured all over the road and the creature. The creature lifted her body, letting her blood pour into its mouth and coat its upper body with the slick liquid. An iron stench filled the air as it began snapping her limbs and ripping them off to eat them as if they were crab legs. Bones popped and flesh ripped whenever the creature tore off a new part and bit into it. The creature's orange eyes glowed in the night.

I lay there ready to accept my fate. I took one last breath, expecting to be once again assaulted by the iron smell of my friend's blood, but it wasn't iron I smelled. It was gasoline. A strange emotion then took over. A sense of hope, but also a sense of pure fury. I now saw a way to kill this monster; this monster who had taken my childhood wonder of the forest and twisted it into something horrid, this monster who had killed my friends in front of me. In those moments I no longer felt fear, dread, or hopelessness. I only felt the pure urge to kill.

I tried to get out of the car as quickly and as quietly as I could. I took out the box of matches from my pocket that I had used to start the campfire. I lit the match and as the creature rushed toward me, I threw the match into the pool of gasoline and watched in vengeful terror.

The flames spread and then covered the creature. It roared in pain as it stumbled and tried to put out the flames before running into the woods. I ran away as fast as I could when I realized the car was about to catch fire too. An explosion went off in the distance before my energy ran out and my broken body gave out as everything went black.

I woke up in a hospital. I'd been picked up by a passing driver. I told people my story but they didn't listen. They said it was the trauma playing tricks on me since they believed I survived a bear attack and the forest fire. I stayed with my parents while I recovered, grateful that it was over. One night later that creature came to me in my dreams, and I saw what it had done to Sam and Gabe. When Gabe went to the bathroom that thing found him. It must have snuck up on him from behind and jabbed its claws through his back before biting down on his head and ripping it off. As for Sam, it attacked him viciously, ripping him to shreds, making his body unrecognizable as if his body was made of tissue paper.

I woke up in a cold sweat after the dream, crying my eyes out, thinking of my lost friends. I opened my window for some fresh air, hoping it would calm me down. A sense of shock seeped into my brain when I could've sworn a dark shadow moved across the window. The shadow wasn't that of a passing animal or a tree swaying, but of a long, dark hand.

I would never see my friends again. No new memories would ever be made with them. I'd never hear Gabe's stupid jokes or reminisce with Sam. I'd never see Odisia smile or explore the possible relationship we could've had.

I cried like a child into my pillow for what felt like a millennium before taking in a shaky deep breath and wiping my tears. I never knew emotional pain could be that intense. It was like an ocean, impossibly deep and vast, and nothing around for miles. You look in all directions and yet there's no living thing in sight and you're left alone in the void. It slowly crawls into your throat, your stomach, and your lungs, suffocating you until you perish in a well of quiet suffering witnessed by no one, and yet painful enough to kill millions.

I sniffled softly and slowly calmed myself down, hoping desperately that this pain would end someday. But fate would not have it. I nearly collapsed and died on the spot when I heard the soft sound of Odisia's voice.

"ERIC...I'M HERE."

BURNING ICE

I RAN THROUGH MY burning village, people were screaming at every turn, crying and begging for help. They were crying out in pain and agony as their flesh melted from their bones and they pleaded for God to save them, but there was no God there. I ran down the cobblestone road with fire surrounding me. The flames engulfed and devoured the straw roofs of every home in the village. The fire crawled like dying men through the roads, reaching out desperately for another home to burn. I had to get home, I knew that I had to get home, that was all that was on my mind. No matter the cost, no matter if the whole village was consumed by flame around me. I was almost there but that's when the worst of it started.

Creatures began to crawl out of the flames, horrifying creatures that were at least eight feet tall. They had teeth that were made out of blades, razors, and other sharp weapons, many of them had also wrapped themselves in barbed wire. The wire tore and ripped up their flesh, burning blood seeping from the cuts. Blood so hot that it could burn holes in the flesh of any living thing it touched. These lacerations didn't slow them down. If anything it seemed to excite them. The pain sent them into a euphoric frenzy that could only be satiated in blood. They began to move through the city like a plague of locusts, destroying what little buildings weren't on fire and attacking those who escaped the flames of damnation. My dread only increased after seeing these horrid creatures. I did everything in my power to avoid their hellish gaze, trying my best to move between the still-burning homes. It took all my strength to keep myself from coughing as the black smoke filled my lungs. The thought of my family, and getting them out of this hell was the only thing that gave me such strength.

They used their blade-filled mouths to tear the flesh of the innocent. As I ran, I saw one remove the barbed wire from its scared body and wrap it around a person's neck, before hanging them with it. I quickly moved behind a charred pile of wood that used to be a house, the smell of burnt wood still fresh in the air. The poor soul who was being hung gagged and desperately tried to remove the wire but it was no use. Blood oozed and gushed from his neck and killed him in a second. The demons cheered like wild animals as they let the blood drip onto their bodies and into their mouths. While they cheered and danced, a few began to chant in some hellish language that I couldn't understand. Even so, I felt the words burn my ears. I let out a small scream from the pain. I quickly covered my mouth and prayed they hadn't heard me, but as I said, there was no God there.

They let out a chorus of demonic laughter as they began to pursue me. It would be obvious to even a child that they were faster. It was nothing but sport to them, letting me outpace them to keep their morbid game going. They enjoyed the chase, and the fear that replaced the blood in my veins added to their fiendish pleasure. The black smoke I'd been inhaling was catching up with me. My legs grew weak and I coughed so hard I thought my throat would be torn to pieces. Just in time, the demons became bored and began to hasten their pursuit.

Thinking quickly, I turned into one of the burning houses. The center support beam had been weakened by the flames. Perfect. I waited for them to get closer, their bloodlust clouding their minds from my plan. I kicked the pillar, causing it to snap and collapse part of the house, crushing the creatures beneath it.

I quickly left the building, not wanting the rest of the house to collapse on me. I didn't linger, not losing sight of my goal. I had to get home to make sure my family was alright. They had to be alright. I reached my home and, curiously, it was the only thing that wasn't burned. I quickly ran inside and called out their names, desperately hoping they were okay, but I couldn't find them anywhere. Suddenly the air felt cold, so unbelievably cold. I shivered as I turned around to look at my front door. Out of everything that happened, gazing into his eyes is what I regret the most. My soul itself froze as he calmly walked in as if he were a man returning home.

He had a smile on his face that looked like he was seeing an old friend. He wore a cloth of pure white, but the edges of the fabric were lined with silver. As he walked further, ice formed wherever he stepped, with small blue flames around the formation.

"Where is he now," he asked, "that all-knowing, all-powerful one that you pray to? Where has he gone?" His voice stung as if poison was dripped into my ear with each word. "The endless love now comes."

"Where is my family," I asked trying to sound brave, but instead I sounded like a small pup.

"Where they need to be. Where they deserve to be." It was so cold that it felt like the air itself was freezing.

"Bring them back," I managed to stutter out.

He smirked, "You know that isn't how this works. But do not worry little one, you'll be reunited for eternity."

"Where?"

"Now why would I spoil the fun? The look you'll show us when you find out will be delightful." A bright, blue halo formed above his head as his smile stretched across his cheek, revealing teeth that looked sharp enough to cut a diamond. The sounds of bones snapping could be heard as bloodstained white wings sprouted from his back. In a voice that dripped with beautiful anguish, he said, "I have such sights to show you."

THE FLAMING BALLERINA

THE ICY WIND HOWLED through the trees, feeling like tiny daggers stabbing into my cheeks. "I knew I should've worn my larger scarf," I mumbled as I walked up to one of the trees at the edge of the forest that surrounded my cabin. The wind kept blowing, making the leafless trees dance and the white ground swirl as if the two were trying to outdo each other. I tightened my grip on my axe then took a hard swing at the base of the closest tree. The trees there were strong and always took several hard swings to chop down. I couldn't complain too much since the hard work helped me keep warm on those dark, cold days.

The world felt so much smaller there. My cabin stood in a clearing, protected by trees on all sides and the closest cabin was several miles away. It was like I was on my own planet, and that's just how I liked it. We often underestimate the quiet, and how comforting it can be. In a lifetime of constant noise and being suffocated by our fellow man, we forget the peace that blissful silence can bring.

The only sounds that day were the wind, the chopping of wood, and nature's dancers. Eventually, after several hard swings from my axe, the tree gave way and fell to the ground with a mighty thud, making snow fly into the air. *Crack.* Another sound of nature, and the noise that wood makes when being split with an axe. I had refined this art of splitting wood to perfection. I could bring my axe down on the dead center of the log with the exact amount of force needed to split it with one chop. *Crack. Crack. Crack.* I paused for a moment. The last one didn't split completely. I stared at it with a strange sense of curiosity, like a child seeing something for the first time.

"Getting sloppy, old man." I grabbed the partially split log with both hands and pulled it apart. To make bringing the logs home easier, I tied them together and placed the piled on a sled. This also ensured no log would ever be left behind. I despised wasting the gifts that nature provided me. Some would be used as firewood, some would be used for carving, and some I'd make into useful tools or furniture. "Be kind to the world, and the world will then be kind to you in return."

These trees have provided me with everything I own, from the cabin I live in, to the hilt of my axe. Now they'd give me the wood I needed to get through the long, cold winters that my area was famous for.

The fire crackled in the small fireplace of my living room, providing a calming melody. I saw another one of nature's dancers in the flickering flames. They moved so elegantly, like ballerinas who had practiced their entire lives just to put on this fiery display. I don't know if it was the sound, the dancing, or the combination, but I ended up falling asleep while watching the fire.

When I woke up the fire was still going. I must have not been out for very long. I was about to go get myself some dinner when a flicker of fiery movement caught my eye. The way the fire danced now was different from before. I looked closer and couldn't believe the image I saw. I even rubbed my eyes and squinted to make sure nothing was playing tricks on me but there was a woman made of flame dancing in the fire. I stood up to get a closer look. She was a ballerina doing a dance routine on the log. She jumped and spun on her toes, moving with such an elegant grace I had only seen in nature. When my knees hit the floor I realized I had moved closer to the fire.

I was entranced and astonished by the movements of the girl, so much so that I was now mere inches from the flames. The orange flames moved with the grace of falling snowflakes, and the heat washed over my face like rolling waves. The ballerina stopped dancing and looked at me. She smiled sweetly and placed her hands on my cheeks, causing a slight burning sensation on my flesh. The burning offered sweet relief and I found myself unable to turn from her gaze.

"You have honored this forest well," she said, her voice calm and peaceful. "Be kind to the world, and it will be kind to you." She pulled me closer and kissed my lips. The burning intensified as I accepted her kindness. It was as though I was slowly burning away, but also being reborn. "Until the next time we meet."

When she finished speaking the flames burned a vast array of different colors, filling the room with varying colors of light. The flames burned like this for a few seconds before quickly extinguishing, replacing the wondrous colors with a calm dimness. I suddenly gasped, realizing I hadn't taken a breath throughout the whole experience. I quickly touched my face and lips. Everything was intact and the burns were no longer there, but the feeling of being reborn remained. I felt rejuvenated and full of energy.

Outside the window, it was now pitch black even though it was early afternoon when the flaming woman appeared. The trees were still dancing as the wind blew through them.

"What a wonderful night it is." I smiled as I grabbed my coat and stepped onto my porch. I took in a deep breath of the winter air and sat down on my rocking chair. "What a wonderful night indeed."

At Least We Tried

I RAN OUT OF food last week. I searched for more in the nearby town. I looked in the nearby houses that were once home to families, but just like the families, the food had vanished long ago. I traced my hand along the rotting wooden walls. The wood made a soft groaning noise, as years of neglect had taken its toll. It was strange to see a home outlive its family. It was as if the home itself was begging to die.

Finding no food at any of the homes, I moved to the supermarket. The sign that once displayed the name of this place was nowhere to be seen. "What are you called again?" I asked. Much like a school child who forgets the information they never use, I too had forgotten this unused information.

Getting no response from the store, I headed inside. There was a sense of melancholy in the air. Some lights hung from their cords, while others flickered, struggling to stay alive just like me. "If you can do it, so can I," I said as I browsed the shelves. Unfortunately, this place was empty too. "Oh well, at least I tried."

My stomach growled as I walked through the broken and ruined city. My travels brought me to the once lush park that sat in the center of the city. This place used to be so grand and beautiful, a place where children laughed, played, and made fond childhood memories that would stay with them for years to come. This is where people used to go to get away from the stress of the world. The massive, circular park stretched five miles from one end to the other and was a proud beacon of the city. Now it was nothing more than a reminder that everything dies. The grass had gone from an emerald green covering all part of the park to scattered brown splotches. The trees, once lush, alive, and full of leaves, were now either barren or had fallen over. A park once full of ambient sounds of birds and woodland animals was now encased in a deafening silence; the kind that surrounds you in a void, the kind that even though you can see everything around you, it still seems as if nothing exists. The one universal constant that ties every living thing together is that one way or another we all rot and decay. At least they had tried to save it when this all started.

After the explosion, things went bad quickly. The people of this city tried desperately to keep the forest alive, but it seemed like the air itself was killing it. They did everything they could but, in the end, it wasn't enough. People started to lose hope when the trees started to die. It was a constant reminder that they could meet the same fate. They spiraled down a hole of insanity as everything crumbled around them. Many tried to fly away after that by jumping from the buildings. But I never saw any of them fly. They all hit the ground hard and didn't get back up. I'd like to think some flew away though, that they found a better place and were laughing again. I miss their laughter the most. I'd never consume food again if that would bring back the laughter of the people that use to play in the park.

Continuing on my travels, I found a dead man laying up against a building, surrounded by the bodies of beasts that had torn apart his body. He was holding some sort of rifle. I attempted to remove the rifle from his hands, but even in death, he had an iron grip. "Easy brave one, I only wish to inspect it," I said as I pried the gun away from him. The empty magazine must've been spent on the animals that I think used to be dogs, but had now mutated beyond recognition. I pulled out a clip of ammunition from my bag and placed it on the body of the dead man, along with his gun. He had run out of ammo in this life and I didn't want him to go into the next life with an empty gun. "At least you tried to live. That's more than most can say, my friend."

I zipped up my pack and continued my lonely walk through a narrow ally with floors of cobblestone. A cool breeze pushed against my face and grazed my ears as if the world was whispering beautiful sorrows to me.

The narrow alley opened to another street. As I looked around to see what sort of buildings sat on this street I saw someone. Another dead someone, but still a someone. The person was young, couldn't have been more than ten. It was a little girl with red hair in a pink dress with little animals on it. She was face down on the road with her arms and legs stretched out as if she had been trying to fly. A strange way to die for one so young. This strange sight made me investigate further, which eventually led me to look straight up at the buildings.

One of the buildings had a short platform that led to nowhere. It appeared to be a platform for people to jump from. I almost tried that too when I was a child. I wanted to fly like Superman, fly like a hero.

"Are you a hero, little one?" I lifted her face to allow her to speak, but when I got a good look at her face I quickly placed it back down. Silly me. I had forgotten that the dead don't talk. I then remembered why I never jumped. My parents stopped me before I could try.

"Where are your parents, little one?" I went into the building, guessing they had to be close by but I couldn't find them on any of the floors. It was so quiet you would have never guessed that hundreds of people used to work in this now-quiet building.

The only place that was left to check was the roof, but I didn't expect to find them there. If they had been there they would have seen their child about to jump and they would have stopped them. But when I opened the door to the roof I found them there. Two corpses. One a man, the other a woman.

"Are you who I'm looking for?" I asked while I looked over their bodies. The man wore a small, gold necklace. I gently removed it and upon closer inspection, saw that it could be opened. Inside, there was a small picture of who I assumed to be the man and the woman sitting before me. However, in the picture, there was also a little girl with red hair. Her parents now lay there, next to the edge of the building, dead like her.

Now more curious than ever, I looked them over to see how they could've died. I found holes in their heads and an old gun lying beside them. Their bodies looked more decayed than the girl's, so they must've died first. They left her alone in a world where a child couldn't survive. Didn't they know people are supposed to take care of your children?

I walked over to the platform the child jumped from and looked at the body lying down below. "At least you tried to fly. At least you tried to be a hero." Maybe I would try to fly again someday.

I suddenly felt very tired. I'd gone too long without eating again. Cutting my scavenging short, I went back to the street in search of somewhere secure to rest my head. "I've been surviving for this long, I hate for one of those mutant dogs to end it after all this."

The next building was a shelter— or what was left of one. It was broken, just like everything else. People had flocked to these when the horror all started. I would know. I was in one too, one just like this. Mine collapsed as well. There was screaming then, a lot of screaming. Did these people scream too? Maybe they knew what was coming and were silent.

I walked into what was left of the building and found two more people. Two dead people, but still people. Their bottom halves had been crushed by rubble and their top halves were holding onto each other. They must've loved each other. I loved someone in my shelter too. My daughter, a light that shined brighter than a star. When our water rations were handed out at the beginning of each week she always asked, "Did the other kids get water too, Daddy?" Such a loving soul she was, making the children happy by playing games with them, and making sure they had enough food and water. So young and yet so caring. Stuck in a world so dark and yet she shined so bright. But as I said, we're all united in a single way. In a world gone mad, even lights decay.

Something happened on the surface that day and the shelter shook. People started to scream again, just like they did when the first signs showed. Pushing, clawing, punching, and kicking to try and get out. We had all desperately made our way to this shelter to escape the world outside, and now we were killing each other to try to get back to it. I kept my daughter close, telling her to hold onto me no matter what happened. She listened and held onto me. Through swarms of frantic people, she never let go. She still shined even as our sanctuary came crumbling down around us.

As we made our way through, another rumble came from the surface, and parts of the shelter fell next to us. I was okay, and my daughter's hand was still wrapped around mine. She felt lighter though, a lot lighter, and when the dust cleared, I saw why. She was buried under the rock, but still held onto me, just like I had told her. Such a good girl, holding onto her daddy no matter what. If I had been closer to her, we would've been like the two holding onto each other in front of me. "At least we tried to stay together."

I felt my knees collide with the hard concrete in front of the dead couple and I let out a scream of anguish. This mental defense I'd put up came crashing down. I tried to numb everything I'd felt, tried to make myself lose a bit of sanity or just not care so I wouldn't be completely ruined. But what was the point of that? Why was I even still here? I questioned all of this as I screamed and slammed my fist onto the floor. "Why do I try? What was it all for?"

I started to climb up the rubble, pieces of it falling onto the ground below. My hand nearly slipped off, but I was able to regain my footing. "Can't fly yet, not high enough."

I eventually reached the top of the building. There was a calming breeze that brushed past my ears again. I looked up to the rising sun, the first one I'd seen since this all started. The gray clouds parted and revealed explosions of oranges, reds, yellows, and purples.

I knew this sky. This was the same masterpiece given to me when I first brought my daughter, my light, home. I was convinced that part of the sky was used to make her. I had no other explanation for how something so beautiful could exist. Under those colors, she gripped my finger tightly in her small hands. She was everything I ever wanted in a daughter, everything I wanted in life.

I sat down, tears flowing down my cheeks like a river flowing down a hill, and watched the sunrise. Filled with the foreign emotion of calm, I was brought back to better days.

"At least I tried."

THE GODDESS OF DEATH

I ALWAYS VIEWED THIS world as nothing short of beautiful, filled with life and love. I always stood in awe at how complicated yet peaceful it all seemed. A network of trees and underground roots, all seamlessly connected as if it were all planned by an expert architect. Animals eating and hunting in a delicate balance, the natural order of things keeping control of the population as if some unseen force was directing existence itself to make sure everything flowed perfectly. These factors all merge and flow to make a beautiful symphony that has been loved and worshiped by cultures worldwide for generations. But behind the curtain of beauty, there is a play of horror.

There are Gods and Goddesses in this world who lie in secret and pull the strings of existence so that it fits their image. One of these Goddesses is named Absoloth, the Goddess who has two sides to her. One side is responsible for all the life that one sees before them. The plants, the animals, and even you and me are all crafted and molded by her out of the components of the universe. In this form, she appears as the most beautiful female one could imagine. Her other form, however, is something far more sinister and dark.

I saw her for myself when I went on an expedition to Iron Wood Park in Minnesota. I was a professor at Draco University and I was researching local plant life for my class lectures. While I was walking through the thick woods, however, I tripped over an exposed root sticking out of the dirt. It sent me careening to the ground, and my spine crashed against a rock. A sickening crunch followed by a wave of numbness flooded through me. Darkness quickly took me. My world crumbled, faded away, and I was taken to a large forest. The length of this forest seemed infinite in both distance and beauty. The trees were so tall and looked so healthy, as if every one of them got the perfect amount of water and sunlight and was planted in the perfect soil. The animals were like nothing I'd ever seen. I saw animals from our world, but also creatures that were foreign in every sense of the word. Creatures with blue bodies at least 40 feet long, and dozens of legs. They were cuddly and seemed curious about my presence. There were also deer with impossibly large antlers, birds bigger than pterodactyls, and whales that swam through the air. At the center of it, was a tree that dwarfed everything else. This tree was so massive that if you flew into space, you'd be able to see it perfectly and protrude off the planet. It was as if I had been given perfect peace, and I felt as though I could stay there for eternity. It felt as though I had spent hundreds of thousands of years there, however, the peace did not last.

It all began to crumble to dust and blow away right before my eyes, the massive tree being the last thing to fade away. I was swallowed up by an eternity of darkness that had only one other entity. That entity was Absoloth. She was as big as the tree at the center of the forest, her eyes as black as the very space around us, and her face a mixture of black and white. Her neck and face were mostly white but black surrounded her eyes and jaw making it look like her skull was visible. I couldn't tell if this was her natural skin or makeup, or if it was genuinely her skeleton. Her long white hair looked as if it was made out of the wind itself. She was beautiful until she opened her eyes.

What I thought were eyes were just her eyelids and when they opened, they revealed silver orbs that showed me the life and death of anything that had ever lived. Every painful death cut my very soul into pieces as her jaw unhinged like some hellish serpent. The dark abyss that was her mouth opened, revealing a demonic green inferno. The sliced-up pieces of my soul pulled out of my very being and into the flames. I screamed in agony. It was as though my body was being torn apart atom by atom, like all that I was and ever would be was tearing away.

It was the worst pain imaginable, and I felt it for years. I begged for death within the first ten minutes. After an unknown number of years in this new world, I finally felt the end coming. My very essence would soon be lost to the void of infinity. But then, the pain suddenly stopped, and I felt my being slowly return to my body. I looked at Absoloth. She had taken the form of a beautiful woman with long, raven black hair, and crystal green eyes that looked as though they were crafted from emeralds. Her skin was fairer and clearer than the Blue River of Greenland.

She smiled shyly at me. "You have endured much, but it doesn't end here for you." Her voice sounded like it came from every conceivable place in the void, as though she was the void and, in turn, the void was her. "It appears it is not yet your time. Though death wrapped you in its grasp, you have escaped it. I'll see you soon."

I woke suddenly with a sharp pain in my back and was surrounded by bright lights. They assaulted my unadjusted eyes, and I couldn't feel anything below my waist. I panicked, thinking that the void was taking hold of me again, but then I heard voices. My eyes adjusted and I saw normal ceiling lights. The voices belonged to doctors marveling over the fact that I was still alive. They told me I'd been found in the woods, on the verge of death. I had been unconscious in the woods for two days before I was found. Luckily, they were able to save my life. Unfortunately, I was paralyzed from the waist down.

After a long process of rehab, I was finally able to walk again, but even though my body healed, my mind never fully did. I never looked at nature quite the same way. It still brought me peace but I was constantly afraid of that peace being taken away. I was terrified of death, of seeing Absoloth again, and it began to affect how I lived my life. I lost sleep, always in fear I'd drift back to the void if I shut my eyes too long. I always had to have some kind of noise. If it got too quiet, I could faintly hear Absoloth's voice. In my dreams, I'd be standing in front of the tree, its massive trunk eclipsing everything around me. It only got worse when the dreams turned into hallucinations that plagued my reality.

I never told anyone what I saw. How could I? No one would believe a word and, even if they did, they'd dismiss it as some hallucination brought on by a near-death experience. My work at Draco University was affected as well. I rushed through lessons and found far less passion, joy, and beauty in my work. The parks of Iron

Wood only brought a sense of paranoia. 'Is that tree here? Are these smaller ones surrounding us its spawn?' I'd wonder. A few kind-hearted students would ask me what was wrong, but I turned them away like I did everyone else. If I'd told them the truth, they'd think I was crazy. If they didn't think me crazy and believed me, I feared they would be sent down the same pit I was cast into.

As the years passed, I began to fear the outside. Whenever I was around living things I felt a strange presence, something more than what I was seeing in front of me. At first, I just felt it around animals, but then it happened with plants. Eventually, I could even feel it with the insects. As soon as I could sense it around people I quit my job. I could hardly function in public areas.

One day, I had gone out for a coffee in hopes of calming down, but horror gripped me when the barista handed me my coffee. Everyone had Absoloth's eyes, those bleak eyes that no light could escape. Then everyone had her voice. Whenever someone spoke, I could hear their voices everywhere at once.

I screamed and dropped my coffee. "Just leave me alone!"

Everyone looked at me, confused.

"I'm not dead... I'm not dead," I repeated over and over.

A woman suddenly spoke, louder than the others. "Are you alright, sir?" She had the face of Absoloth, and green flames surrounded her

"Stay away! Don't take me," I screamed as I ran out of the coffee house and back to my home as fast as I could. I became a shut-in, leaving my house only when I was completely out of food, and when I did so, I never looked into anyone's eyes.

That's where Absoloth is, in their eyes, for they are the windows to your soul. She's part of every living thing since all life comes from her. She waits behind the window, seeing all that you are, always a part of you until it's time to take back the soul she gave you. She is all we are and all we ever will be. She's the tree at the center of it all.

As I neared my end, her grasp began to take hold of me. Her grip slowly tightened as I grew closer and closer to the abyss. I knew what awaited me, green flames and a monster that had every living thing in the palm of her hand. I felt death slowly come over me, washing over me a tide that slowly got deeper and deeper, washing over my whole body until I was completely submerged and fell into the endless sea of darkness.

There was no escape. I was drowning. Drowning in a sea of life and death, suffocating in an air of humanity. It surrounded and gripped me, binding and restricting me like millions of hands had taken hold of me and were dragging me away from life and towards death. I felt stuck in an endless sea of limbo and uncertainty, as if a swarm of insects had descended upon me, covering me with thousands of legs, crawling around outside and inside my skin. Berated by constant static that seemed to get louder and louder, I screamed in pain and horror until I was sure my ears would rupture and my vocal cords would tear.

"Mercy! Mercy!" I called out. Though no matter how loudly I screamed, this sea drowned all sounds. I was a helpless organism in a cosmic sea of suffering beyond my human understanding that showed no signs of ending. Then inexplicably, the torture abruptly ended, and I found myself back in the forest.

But what was once a peaceful paradise for me became a personal hell. I was constantly surrounded by beings who had the essence of Absoloth, except the essence was far stronger this time. The same creatures who had once brought me joy only brought fear and dread. I had no escape from them now. It was torturous. I was continually reminded of my inevitable fate. I spent every second of those hundreds of thousands of years thinking of the ghastly woman and the green inferno that awaited me. When I saw that massive tree in the center of the forest again, my brain spiraled into chaos and agony.

All that time destroyed me mentally. The long creatures with many legs attempted to cheer me up but their attempts were in vain. Eventually, closing my eyes made it tolerable. Hearing their soft coos and feeling their soft, warm bodies against mine brought me a small amount of peace for the first time in 200,000 years. I had even managed to smile when I realized that the presence of Absoloth was not only death but life too. Those living creatures that had brought me joy had her essence. When I saw her eyes and heard her voice at the coffee shop, I was seeing the small piece of herself she gives to every one of us. Even this fuzzy creature in my arms was a living thing and had her essence. So did all other things—including me. Her presence wasn't something to fear. It was just a constant, an interweaving thread that connects us all through consciousness. We are Absoloth and she is us, the essence of creation and life itself, all made from a single source. So many varieties of life and culture, all originating here, at a single point.

I eventually settled into my madness, and finally accepted all that would happen. When the world around me crumbled once again I did not fight, I did not scream, and I did not beg like a newborn. I gave all the creatures one last goodbye and then fell into the endless abyss once again. However, this time the dark did not feel like millions of insects. It felt like water. Clean, beautiful water that carried me gently, like slowly flowing down a stream. It was comforting and calm and, unlike last time, I no longer feared what was at the end of the journey.

I eventually reached the end of the long, winding stream of darkness, and before me, stood Absoloth. But she wasn't a black-and-white woman with long white hair and bones for skin. She was the fair-skinned, raven-haired, emerald-eyed woman I had seen at the end of our last meeting.

"I see that you're ready now." She smiled and stepped toward me. "Do you have any regrets?" Her eyes locked onto mine.

I was unable to look away or lie to the woman standing before me. "My only regret is that I feared you for so many years and wasted so much time fearing something that is only natural."

She gave me another smile and a satisfied nod. "A good lesson to learn for next time." I was about to ask her what she meant but she shook her head. "Don't worry about it now, just sleep." She kissed me, and I felt all I was fade away, drifting calmly across a sea of life and death, searching for something new. "See you again soon."

FRELSARI

WHY ARE YOU HERE? What draws you to this knowledge? Curiosity, entertainment, boredom? What draws you to keep learning about these deities that make your life a hell purely for entertainment? I suggest you ponder that question as you keep learning more.

Of course, there are not only deities who inhabit the plane of existence they dwell in. There are also the creatures that carry your soul to these deities and they are called Frelsari. Now we all know how these creatures operate. When you die they come to you and carry your soul to the next plane of existence. We also know that when Frelsari come into our world they will appear as a crow, however, unlike normal crows, they can't be killed no matter what you do to them. You can shoot them and they won't flinch, stab them and they won't resist, however good luck finding one. They are far more intelligent than typical crows. They won't fall for any trap that you or anyone else can conceive and will never get close enough for you to grab them. There is only one way that you can tell the difference between a Volitar and a real crow. A Volitar won't caw or make any noises at all when it sees you. It will only glare at you, making sure that you're 'their' person. This simply means that they are your Volitar, the one that takes your soul when you perish from this plane. You'll find that creatures of such intelligence are hardly ever wrong.

Do not be afraid. This doesn't mean you'll die once they set their eyes on you. It just means that you will die one day as almost all things do one way or another. When that day arrives, they will take your soul to the plane where these deities exist and their true forms are revealed. They could appear as winged humanoids that look very much like demons with sharp teeth-like razors, and claws that are longer and sharper than any dagger. These are the claws they use to carry your soul.

Or maybe they'll appear as a heavenly angel holding you gently as you're whisked on a stream of silk. It all depends on the person, but not for the reasons you may think. Good luck figuring out those reasons though. No one else has ever figured it out. As all-knowing as these beings and the gods they serve are, they have never once been known for their clarity. They simply deposit your soul at its determined destination and go back to the world of the living, waiting for the next soul to die. The work of a Volitar is never done, not until the last star in this grand plane of existence is extinguished.

BEWARE THE DRAUGR

MY MOTHER AND FATHER always told me grand tales of the Gods. Thor facing mighty Frost Giants, or how Týr did not so much as flinch when the giant wolf, Fenrir, bit off his hand as retribution after the Gods tricked him. Tales of bravery, might, wonder, and glory that the Gods and warriors of old had achieved. These stories are meant for children's ears, for those who have not yet learned the darker secrets that this world holds deep in its history. It was only when I grew older when the hair on my face had only just begun to grow, did my parents tell me the darker tales.

"That's good, my son," my father said when I blocked his attack with my shield. Both my parents had been teaching me how to fight ever since I grew strong enough to hold an axe.

"Perhaps one day I'll be better than you, Father," I said, confidently puffing out my chest.

My father chuckled. "Perhaps you will. Though I hope you don't get as good as your mother, or the Gods themselves will have something to fear." He lowered his Damascus sword and wooden shield. "That's enough for now. We should rest for a bit." I nodded and sat down with him, sweat dripping down my brow. We both began to eat some of the cooked meat we had brought with us.

"Father, could you tell me the tale of when Thor and Loki encountered the giant Utgard-Loki again?"

He laughed "Your mother and I must have told you that story a thousand times by now."

"I can't help it. It's one of my favorites. Hearing how Thor can lift part of Jörmungandr and make the ocean shrink with just a few gulps gives me strength."

My father laughed again but the smile faded. "Son, those stories are good and you should be inspired by them. However, the ones you know often leave out the darker parts of what we defend ourselves against."

I looked at him confused. "Father, I already know about many of the monsters."

"Yes, you do, but you do not know what they truly are. You know of their existence, yes, but you lack the knowledge of just how terrifying an encounter with them can be." He paused and got a faraway look in his eye.

"Father?"

He shook his head slightly then put his arm around my shoulder. "Son, I think it's time I tell you some of the darker parts of this world."

His hold on me tightened as if he was trying to protect me from something. He told me many things on that day: why the Jotnar are so terrifying, how they have a strength that rivals the Gods, how if they were to ever kill the Gods humanity would surely end, and if Jörmungandr ever let go of his that it would be the beginning of Ragnarök, the end of all things. But for some unknown reason, the thing my father told me that day that stayed with me the most was the Draugr.

The Draugr used to be a regular person, full of wants and needs. But now, a Draugr is a regular person trapped in a state that is not quite life but also not quite death. These undead are husks of their former selves, with their decaying skin peeling off and exposing their bones. Their eyes (those who had them) often glowed an icy blue.

I asked my father, "How do you know if someone will become a Draugr after they die?" He told me that people who were wicked or overly greedy could become Draugr, such as those who hoarded the spoils of a raid or let their fellow man starve while they had a full belly. It only makes sense that a person that is wicked and greedy enough to do that would also be greedy enough to stay in this world when they are supposed to pass on to the next.

"If you ever see a corpse that is not laying down on the ground, then make sure that it is dead, son. If it is not, then it could be a Draugr resting or playing dead."

My hands had begun to shake at that point.

"The Draugr are angry that we get to live while they have to die and, with their infinite greed, they wish to take the lives away from those that still have it."

We finished our food and went back to training, but I couldn't get the image of the Draugr out of my head. I think my father realized this since he stopped our training earlier than usual. He told me that he had never personally seen a Draugr and that people around here knew the myths and were not foolish or greedy enough to become Draugr. This put me at ease slightly.

That night I was sleeping in my bed, the animal fur blanket warm and soft, shielding me from the cold air that howled outside. In the infinite darkness of my sleep, however, a soft, elegant voice spoke to me "Your father is right." The voice scared me so much I couldn't move or talk "Beware the Draugr, for they are tied to your fate."

A hand touched my forehead and, suddenly, I was outside in my village but not in my own body. I was taller and older. I soon realized that I was seeing all this through the eyes of my father, but everything was burning. The sky was smokey and red embers drifted in the air. Draugr was ripping people apart. People were fighting back but they were soon overwhelmed by the sheer number. Limbs were getting torn off, heads smashed, and organs ripped out of bodies. I tried to help fight them off but I had no control over my body. Against my will, I looked towards the sea. A boat of people with blurred faces reached out for me as if they wanted to take me with them. Then I saw a pair of icy blue eyes staring directly at me.

I shot up from my bed, heaving air. It felt like I had been holding my breath for several minutes. Sweat as cold as the ice on a frozen lake flowed down my cheeks and dripped onto the floor. For a second, I could hardly tell where or who I was. I tried to spot the Draugr I had just seen in front of me. But there was no Draugr to be seen. Had it been a dream? It felt so real, I could still smell the smoke of the burning homes and hear the screams of people getting ripped apart, but here I was, in my body, in my bed, completely safe.

My mother came into my room and sat at the edge of my bed. "What's wrong my little warrior?" She placed her hand on my cheek. Her hand, so soft and gentle, instantly made me feel calm and safe from anything that could happen.

"I had a horrible nightmare, Mother. Draugr came and destroyed our homes and killed so many people. There were people with blurred faces reaching out to me as well, but I don't know what they wanted." We hugged, and I finally felt safe with her arms around me.

"Don't worry my child. If Draugr ever came here your father and I would protect you." She looked into my eyes and smiled. "Besides, by the time your father and I finish training you, you will be stronger than any Draugr."

This made me smile and gave me some peace since I knew that she was right. My parents were strong and had gone on many successful raids together. The training they had been putting me through had already made me better than the rest of the young children in our village.

I took my mother's words in stride and began to train harder than ever. Over the years, my skill grew not only in one-on-one fights but also in working with others. This was a good thing since most of our fights and raids involved working together, side-by-side in shield walls. If one man failed the wall could break and that would be the end of all the men. Each man had to be as strong as the one next to them and stronger than the man in front of them.

I went on my first raid when I was fifteen years old, with my mother and father right at my side. Catching the Saxons off guard and letting out screams of fury and victory alongside my parents felt like it was meant to be. The three of us, along with the rest of the raiding party, moved quickly through the small Saxon village, trying to catch them by surprise. We quickly stole what we could and burned what we could not. This would make sure they couldn't recover and mass a counterattack. Once we grabbed everything that we could we quickly brought it back to our longship and got out of there as quickly as possible. Meanwhile, our archers shot arrows at any Saxon fool who tried to catch our ship. Instead of a bit of glory, all they got were arrows to their chests and skulls.

We sang songs and cheered loudly, for we had come away with a plentiful bounty. Many of the other warriors offered congratulations and strong pats on my back, praising me for doing so well on my first raid. What made me feel the proudest, though, were the words my mother and my father spoke.

"Let it be heard that he is my son!" My mother said proudly "Let it be known that it was my womb that grew and my spear that carved him into a warrior."

My father clasped his hand around my forearm. I did the same. A show of respect to each other as warriors. He smiled at me and brought me in for a tight embrace. I returned it. This showed respect as father and son.

My father let out a thunderous laugh and raised my arm in the air. "Let us not forget that this raid was a success because of us all. Let us also not forget that starting on this day, Odin has a new warrior that will eventually join him in his great hall!" The rest of the warriors raised their fists in the air and let out thunderous cheers. 'Tonight we feast and drink until the sun comes up!" This drew an annoyed look from my mother who knew our mead supply would get drained again.

It was about a four-day sail to get back to our home in Norway so we had a bit of time to ourselves. My parents told me stories about their first raid, how my father fell on his face when he first stepped out of the boat, and how my mother managed to get out of it fine, only to realize she had forgotten her sword in the boat. We laughed together and I felt happier than I ever had. If only I could have stayed in that moment forever. If only that wasn't the last time we'd laugh like that together.

About two days into our journey home, we stopped the boat on the coast so we could rest and stretch our legs a bit.

"Hey, come look at this!" one of the men shouted from the nearby woods.

We walked over to him and he pointed to a graveyard. However, the bodies weren't buried. They were all leaning against the trees. They were all very decayed and rotten like they'd been dead for a while. The rest of the men became excited when they discovered the corpses had jewelry on them, an easy opportunity to increase our plunder. At first, I got excited too, but then I saw the look on the faces of my mother and father and remembered the tales that they told me and the dream I had all those years ago.

"I don't think we should disturb the bodies," I said, starting to fear the worse.

One of the men looked at me "Why? It's not like they're gonna need it anymore." He took a ring from one of the boney fingers of the corpse in front of him.

"Look at the bodies. None of them are buried and they're all leaning against the trees. For all we know these could be Draugr," I said. A few of the men and women with us laughed and ignored me.

"The boy is right. We shouldn't tempt fate," my father said.

"Agreed. Doesn't it at least seem strange that the bodies are all leaned up against the trees like this?" my mother added.

This was enough to cause some of the people to change their minds and put back what they took. Others, however, kept looting, one saying, "They are probably like that to keep people who are afraid of their shadows like you away from their jewels." I still thought it was all too strange. I was about to chime in when we heard a scream.

"Let go of me, you rotting bastard!" one of the men yelled. He took out his axe and cut off the hand grabbing him. He fell back and the corpse let out a deep, low groan. Its bones began to creak, its head began to move slowly and stiffly then it let out a loud snap as it stared at us with a pair of icy blue eyes.

"What in Odin's name?" one of our men said

More of the corpses began to wake up one by one. Some of our men were able to escape their cold, dead grasp and help others, but some were not so lucky. The undead pulled them down and tore off their flesh with their hands and teeth. The screams from these unlucky people were the most horrible sounds I'd ever heard. They screamed out for aid, desperate for the undead corpse to stop.

"Quickly everyone, ready yourselves!" my father yelled.

This shook me out of my trance. I quickly grabbed my axe and shield. The rest of the warriors with us did the same. Luckily, the bastards took a while to wake up, allowing those of us who hadn't been killed to brace ourselves for a fight. Thankfully we formed a shield wall in time to stop them. Even though their bodies decayed as much as the dead side of the goddess, Hel's face, their strength was incredible, causing our feet to drag in the mud as they all crashed into us.

"Spears!" my mother called out loudly. Then she and the rest of the warriors who had spears thrust them through the small holes in the wall to stab the undead.

Normal men would fall dead from this, but most of these Draugr roared and reached out with their long, dead fingers, still trying with all their might to take the life from our bodies. The spears pulled back, making some Draugr fall. Their icy blue eyes went dark in some of them but most of them simply continued to push. I heard a scream on the other end of the shield wall. One of our men had fallen. A Draugr quickly fell on top of him and began biting the flesh off of his face. One of the archers standing behind the wall took out his dagger and stabbed the Draugr in the back of the head three times before the foul creature finally fell, but our man was already dead.

"Close the gap," a shield maiden yelled. We quickly moved closer to each other to close the gap that had been made, managing to close it before any more could get through.

"Push," my father yelled. We all pushed as hard as we could. It was like trying to push a mountain, but we managed to start driving them back. My father then yelled, "Archers!" The archers in the back of the wall climbed onto the shoulders of some of the others so they could see over the shield wall. They pulled back their arrows and then let them loose, hitting their targets. The Draugr that had pressed its face right in front of me suddenly found an arrow in its eye and it fell to the ground. A few other Draugr met a similar fate. Their skulls and bodies were pierced with arrows, but some didn't fall. They just rose back up and kept attacking.

"This isn't working!" one of the men said. "We can't permanently keep them all down, and more of the dead keep rising!"

My father nodded and came up with a plan. "Archers, wait for my signal!" He had everyone lock their stance before telling us to use our shields to knock them back. He told those with spears to impale the Draugr. My father then quickly called the archers to let loose another volley. We used this opportunity to back up and get closer to our boats. He repeated this process twice more, but at the cost of two more men. One fell like the previous and another was overwhelmed by three Draugr that had focused on him. We quickly dispatched the ones who broke through before we repeated the process a third time, allowing us enough time to finally get back onto the boat. The archers covered others, firing at will, dropping a few more Draugr as they did so.

The rest of the men and I quickly pushed the boat out deep enough so it could sail and we got in. "Get us out of here," I yelled. Everyone quickly began to row for their lives. I started to relax slightly but then remembered the dream I had so long ago when that mysterious voice showed me a vision of Draugr attacking my village. That never happened. Did I change my fate, or was something even more terrible coming?

The next two days of sailing were quiet. The once loud cheers and songs had faded now that everyone was filled with a heavy sense of dread. Even though the men with me were all battle-hardened warriors, they had never seen something as horrible as what they had just witnessed. They had never seen their friends get their faces eaten off right or their friends get ripped apart as if their limbs were as weak as rotten wood and none of them had ever seen a corpse rise from the dead.

"When they die, they stay dead. When you are stabbed or hit with an arrow you fall and die. Why weren't they dead?" One of the men said quietly to himself. He simply could not understand how the enemy we had faced could have possibly existed.

I knew the feeling all too well. My childhood fear had manifested. My heart began to race and pound so hard that it felt like it was going to explode. My hands and legs began to shake as images of those eyes, those cold, dead, icy blue eyes seemed to stare directly into my soul and destroy me from the inside. I felt like I was about to go completely mad until a familiar hand softly touched my shoulder. The feeling was familiar, calming, and soft. The same hand I would feel after waking up from nightmares as a child, the hand of my mother slowly calming me down as she always did. The look on her face told me everything was going to be okay.

Barely anyone spoke during the entire two-day journey back home. My father was in deep thought as if he was pondering what we should do next, or what events would transpire because of what we had unleashed on that day.

We eventually arrived back home. People cheered but we did not return their cheers. Instead, we gave them looks of regret and shame, knowing we had possibly brought doom upon them all.

"What's wrong?" someone from the crowd asked. "You all look like you're half dead." That statement sent a wave of pain through my heart.

"An evil has awoken," my father said, drawing everyone's attention to him. "An old evil, an evil that has been around since the first people were created. The Draugr are coming." Everyone focused on him. Some had looks of fear and terror, some disbelief, and some doubt.

"Please, if you wanted to play a joke on us all, you could have come up with something better," someone from the crowd shouted. A few of the others chuckled, but my father and the rest of us just glared at him.

"We would not joke about something like this." my mother said. "We disturbed a group of Draugr by. We lost a few people but managed to hold them back long enough to get back to our boats."

My father nodded. "But we didn't kill them all, and now they are angry after being robbed and disturbed. In their infinite greed, they will not stop until they have found us and satisfied their revenge."

Everyone's face instantly paled.

"Do not fear my friends." my father said. "We are proud warriors who have fought countless battles time and time again and we will face this enemy like we would any other."

One of the women in the crowd interrupted. "But we have never faced a foe such as this. Not one who is in between life and death. These foes will not flee in terror or try to save themselves from us when we attempt to take their undead lives."

My father addressed her and anyone else in our village who had doubts. "You speak as if you have always known your enemy as if every time you fought you knew exactly what it would be." He pointed to a man, "Bjorn, did you flee when three hungry wolves attacked you just because you did not expect to fight wolves on that day?"

Bjorn smirked "No, I did not, I held my axe firmly and slew all three of them by myself."

My father nodded, pointing to a shieldmaiden. "And you, Astrid, when your father didn't believe you were strong enough to be a warrior and decided to rip your dreams away by ambushing you, did you abandon your dream because you were not expecting him?"

She chuckled. "No, I kicked his ass!" Everyone laughed.

"And we did not flee when the Draugr attacked us, not even my son who had his first taste of real combat just two days before." A wave of pride washed over me when my father said these words.

"And just like all those times, we will not cower in fear. We will show the Gods that we are all worthy of Valhalla!" My father raised his fists in the air, and everyone joined in and let out a thunderous battle cry.

We began to prepare for the fight of our lives. We put a line of oil in the front of the village as well as set several traps. Our blacksmiths made sure all of our weapons were sharpened and that our shields were sturdy. We spent a few days preparing since the Draugr were traveling on foot, and they would take a while to arrive. They did not need boats to cross the ocean, they could simply walk across the ocean floor. They slowly approach our homes, their anger slowly building with each step.

One day, our scouts came back out of breath. "They're close," one of the men said. "They'll be here by tomorrow night."

The moment we had prepared for had finally come. We made some final preparations and made sure everything was in its right place. That night we gathered and prayed to the Gods to give us strength for the upcoming battle. It would be a battle the likes of which we had never experienced. Some of us, including me, got our faces painted. Those who had chosen to put grooves in our teeth filled the grooves with red dye, making it look like their teeth were bloodstained.

We gathered outside the entrance. Those who were not warriors or simply too young to fight sailed to a nearby island in case the worst happened. My parents stood next to me and calmed my nerves. I was here with them like I had been since I was a young boy. With them by my side every fear I had receded like the tide upon the shore, and I felt as though I could take down the Gods themselves. My mother rested her hand on my shoulder, calming me as she had before. This time, however, she said no words but simply gave me a nod and a smile. I smiled back at her and readied myself for what was about to happen next.

Loud groans came from the woods outside of our village. Groans of desperation and rage seemed to come from the depths of a bottomless pit of anger and despair. Everyone got into their stance, but I could still tell that many of us had fear in our hearts.

"Remember who you are and what you're fighting for," I said, getting everyone's attention. "Show the Gods what you're worth."

The Draugr slowly came over the hill. Their exposed bones creaked, some of their jaws unhinged and they let out an ear-shattering scream that bellowed through the woods. Not to be outdone, we let out a loud battle cry before we formed our shield wall. They began to move towards us. Now that they had been awakened they were able to move much faster than before, some at a jogging pace but some running as if they had trained all their lives.

"Now!" my father yelled. Archers who were standing behind the wall let loose arrows whose tips glowed a flaming orange, and when they pierced the Earth, a wall of fire erupted from the ground.

The Draugr let out screams. Some of them burned away, the blue glow of their eyes slowly fading before they fell to the ground. However, many of them continued, some managing to get through before the fire could fully envelop them. The others pressed on, seemingly ignoring the flames. How greedy could they have been in their lives that they could survive being covered in flames? The archers continued to let loose their arrows, managing to pick off a few more of them before they crashed into us.

"Hold steady!" my mother said, jabbing her spear into one of them. They pushed harder this time, more determined now to destroy our lives, the lives that they no longer possessed.

We tried our best to hold them back, but we got pushed back. More of them piled in. Though the hoard eventually stopped coming, and once the last few piled on, my father yelled out a command and that's when the rest of our hoard came. Roarsenvelop came from close by as if a family of bears had begun to charge. I saw a Draugr get picked up as if it was weightless. It was slammed onto the ground. These were the rest of our warriors who had hidden behind the trees until then. They had taken the undead bastards by surprise and managed to help us turn the tide of battle.

One of our berserkers swung his massive two-handed axe into the waist of one of the Draugr, splitting it in two. Not yet dead, however, it crawled to me and grabbed my ankle. Before I could finish it off myself, the Berserker swung his ax right down the middle of its head. Before I could thank him I smelled smoke from behind me. I quickly turned around and saw that some of the houses had been set alight. A few Draugr had come out of the ocean, tipped over the small pots of oil the archers were using to light their arrows, and turned the fire against us.

One of those Draugr looked directly at me and gave a wide smile filled with rotten teeth. The Draugr began to encircle us while we tried to hold them back. When my father saw the flames he knew that our village was lost and gave the order to make our way to the boats. We stayed close to each other, covering each other's blind spots as we slowly inched our way closer to the boats. The Draugr were being much more aggressive. They would dive on top of the shields, causing some to fall, and those that did were dead before they could even attempt to stand. Their faces were ripped off by decayed teeth, their throats ripped out by long, boney hands, and their organs removed while still alive.

As we neared the boats my legs began to give. A Draugr was hitting my shield over and over again. I was beginning to tire and I felt myself losing my strength.

One of the blows knocked me down to one knee, my axe to the ground. I gritted my teeth, pulled out my short sword, and I jabbed the stomach of the Draugr in front of me. He seemed to let out what I can only describe as a laugh as he grabbed the blade and pulled himself closer, seemingly ignoring the fact that my blade was going further into him. He laughed again, this time close enough for me to smell his rotten breath. The creature pulled back his arm to attack. I tried to pull out my weapon to defend myself, but it was stuck in the Draugr's rotting flesh. I tried to back away, but its ice-cold fingers wrapped around my forearm to keep me in place. He thrust his arm forward, and I felt the searing pain of a thousand suns in my stomach.

My strength fully left me and I collapsed on the floor. There was no grace in how I fell, just a simple mound of flesh falling to the ground. I couldn't move, couldn't feel anything, or say anything.

A bright light and a hand reached out to me and spoke in a soft voice. "You have fought well, young one. Odin wishes to see you in his halls," she said. She was enchantingly beautiful, with long, flowing brown hair, and emerald green eyes that shined like stars. She was wearing chainmail armor, a round shield with a carving of Yggdrasill on it strapped on her back, and a sword with a carving of Odin's spear, Gungnir, on her hip. With no doubt in my mind, I could tell she was one of Valkyrie Odin's warriors who go to battlefields, decide who lives and who dies, then decide where those souls go. If it was any other circumstance, I'd be honored but today was not the day.

"No. I can't go yet. Tell Odin that there is more I must do." I was not about to let my family and fellow warriors go on in this fight without me, but she didn't seem to appreciate my objection.

"It has already been decided. Odin has called for you and the Norns have already weaved it into fate."

I called upon all possible strength I could bring to move my fingers, my feet, then my arms. I forced myself to stand before the maiden warrior, looking at her dead in the eyes. "Tell Odin that there will be a day when I walk in his halls, but it will not be this day."

"You know as well as I that that isn't how this works," she said in a stern tone. "The all father Odin has called for you. You fell gloriously in battle defending your loved ones. There is no shame in accepting the fate laid before you."

"It is an honor hearing such words from a Valkyrie," I said as I straightened my stance. "But I'm not falling on this day."

"You have fallen! Your fate has been woven into time by the Norns themselves. Odin, leader of the Gods has outstretched his generosity to praise you and deem you worthy enough to join him. Your name will be remembered for all time, you shall live in eternal glory, and in the final days you will fight by Odin's side in Ragnarok and you have the gull to deny him?"

"Yes," I said, glaring into her eyes. "Forgive me, Valkyrie, for I mean no disrespect to you or any of the Gods. But I'd rather walk for an eternity in the frozen lands of Niflheim than accept my fate today." She looked at me but I continued "The people of my village are still fighting. They are having their homes burned and people are being slaughtered at the hands of the greedy undead. I cannot allow my people to suffer such a fate. You may attempt to stop me, but I will fight you with everything I have to change my fate. You could bring Thor himself before me, and I'd fight him with my bare hands if it meant saving those that I hold dear." I had defied the Gods and I knew not what would come next, but I had no regrets for what I said.

The Valkyrie grabbed the hilt of her sword and I stood steadfast, preparing for her attack. She took a step forward but stopped. I couldn't tell why at first, but then I heard a soft noise, a breeze. It was slow and gentle, like music. When I listened closer, however, it wasn't music, it was a voice.

"All Father," the Valkyries whispered.

The wind continued to softly blow. I couldn't understand what it was saying, but I didn't need to.

The Valkyrie removed her hand from the hilt of her sword. "Perhaps he gives you more respect than you deserve," she said sternly. A light appeared on her lips. "It appears your fate was not as set in stone as I thought. Do not waste this kindness mortal, for you probably won't be this lucky again." She whistled and a horse as white as fresh snow ran toward us before stopping next to her.

"Then I am to live," I said as she mounted her horse. "When the right time comes, I'll happily accept Odin's offer."

"I'm sure you'll be worth the wait. Go now, don't disappoint us," she said before drawing her sword, raising it, and letting out a shrieking battle cry.

I wasn't on the battlefield anymore. I was laying in a boat. Men were holding back the Draugr while my father pushed out the boat. I managed to relax and lay back. I felt the boat get deep enough to start moving, but my father hadn't gotten in. I saw him staring at me while we drifted further away. I reached out to him, trying to get him to come with us since the Draugr was too far away. Even if he had tried, the Draugr would've caught him due to the water slowing him down. I called out to him but my mother held me back. I screamed and pleaded for him to come. Tears fell my cheeks as black smoke went up into the red sky.

My father raised his hand, smiled, and said, "Make your own story. Become the legends that we told you as a child."

My mother held me down and told me to rest while the others rowed. She was crying as well as she treated my wound.

I never saw my father again after that day but I know that I will see him again in the next life. Until then, I promise that I will slay any undead bastard that dares threaten those I care for. I have begun to tell my children the tales that my parents told me, and one day, I wish to be added to those tales.

AGONY

"MONOTONY," I MUMBLED TO myself, "the monotonous routine of a middle-class man with an office job."

I impaled some of the eggs onto my fork and stared at them. I don't know what I was expecting them to do but I stared, waiting, hoping for something to happen. "I thought so," I said, shoving the eggs into my mouth. After breakfast, I went to work even though my mind was begging me not to. I could hardly stand my job, blankly staring at screens as I typed out reports and filed company documents. My mind defaults to autopilot. If I paid full attention I'd go completely mad.

"They should give this job to war criminals," one of my coworkers said to another. It was a small pleasure to hear that I was not the only one who suffered in this job. But they do always say that misery loves company and, frankly I'm a firm believer in that statement. But it could be worse. The boring routine just gets to me.

Truth be told, I am thankful I have a job that gives me financial security, puts food on my plate, and gives me a roof over my head. I only wish that something more interesting would happen, something to break this horrid routine that I find myself in.

I regretted those words the instant my body was ripped from the world I knew and transported to a world of darkness that no night could ever compare to. It was a madness that would make every politician, murderer, and all the rest seem sane. I pulled my face out of the dirt and discovered I was in a trench. I called out for help, called out for anything, but there was nothing, no noise at all.

I walked inside the trench for a while trying to find something, anything to help me find out where I was. I walked for what must've been for at least an hour, but it seemed like this trench never ended. I looked behind me and everything looked the same as where I had started. Did I somehow imagine walking that distance? I pondered that until a hand grabbed my shoulder.

I recoiled, almost falling over in the process. I'd been grabbed by a person inside of the muddy wall of the trench, except they seemed to be made of the same mud as what was in the trench. The creature groaned as if it was in pain,

"Help!" It groaned and suddenly more arms and faces came out of the mud.

"Light. This one has light in him." another said.

"Please, I'm so cold," begged another.

They all kept trying to grab me and pull me into the mud with them. One managed to grab my arm. Its cold, muddy hand seemed to quickly harden as if it was cement. I slammed all my force against the now hard arm, desperately trying to break it off.

"Your light, give us your light." The voice groaned as it pulled me closer. I could now feel the breath of the muddy people against my face. There was nothing but never-ending darkness in their eyes and mouths.

The cement-like arm finally broke off, causing me to fall to the floor. The mud person screamed so loudly that it felt like my ears were about to bleed. I quickly got up and ran. This time I seemed to be putting some distance between us. I ran until my lungs burned and my legs felt numb before I finally stopped and bent over, heaving to catch my breath. There was still nothing new, however. I was still in the trench, there were still craters all over, and foggy gray mist still surrounded everything.

I heard a loud gust of wind in the distance. It got louder and louder as it grew closer. Then the wind hit me with what seemed like microscopic daggers. My clothes ripped, and my skin tore as I screamed. I covered my face, letting my arms and hands take all the punishment. I begged for it to end. The pain was getting unbearable. I fell to my knees and just as my arms were about to do the same, the wind finally stopped. I panted hard and let out another scream when small amounts of blood trickled down my body.

"Help! Please, anyone!" I called out in vain, desperately wanting to leave this hellish domain.

I limped through the barren land. All I could feel was pain, not only physical but psychological pain. I felt tired and hollow as if my body was slowly fading away. My mind felt like it was slowly fading like I was slowly ceasing to exist like I was becoming just another part of the waste that surrounded me. Empty, uninhabited, void. Time lost its meaning. Seconds felt like hours, and hours felt like the blink of an eye. It had become impossible to tell how far I had walked because I couldn't keep track of where I started. I couldn't count how many steps I had taken either because it seemed like I no longer had feet.

It may have been mere seconds, or it could've been several lifetimes before I looked to the sky for salvation, but what I saw was not salvation. What I saw up there made me wish I was never given the curse of existence. A massive bird was flying above me – or at least a bastardized version of one. It looked half-dead as parts of it were decaying. Instead of normal bird feet, it had several human hands with long talons at the end of each finger that looked sharper than any blade that has been or ever will be crafted. What feathers it had were pure white and elegant, as if it had been expertly groomed. The worst part was a massive, blood-red eye on its stomach. The eye took up the whole torso of the bird and stared directly at me. I somehow knew it could see me, not just the physical me but all my organs, my blood, my life, my soul, my existence. It opened its massive beak and screeched. The sound made me wish I could've spent an eternity in silence. It was an ear-splitting screech, louder than anything on our planet could've been capable of making. Even when my ears burst and my brain lost all thought, I could still hear it. The noise seemed to have no source as if the noise was coming from inside my head. Once I had fallen to the ground it began its dive into me.

I had no strength or will to run away or to try to evade this creature in any way although I desperately wanted to. Every muscle and bone in my body quivered in pure, desperate fear. The creature eventually reached me and the bladed human hands it had for feet grabbed me and began to carry me away. The blades cut into my weak skin, and my blood rained over the desolate, barren plane that I had been existing on. The blood-red iris of the eye moved up to constantly watch me. I screamed and questioned why it kept staring at me. I begged it to blink, to move, to do anything but it just kept staring at me.

The massive bird flew me to a massive tree. The tree was the one beautiful thing that existed in this place. It was full of green leaves and long branches. The tree itself was taller than the tallest building on the planet. It easily pierced the dark clouds and went high above them. The bird flew me to the very top of the tree and dropped me into its nest. The nest had three younger versions of the bird in it, all with different colored eyes on their bodies, all staring at me. Before I could do anything the three birds pounced on me and began to rip my body apart. They ate my flesh, broke my bones, and drank my blood. They fought over my organs and destroyed all that I ever was, tossing my head from the tree when they finished.

I embraced my death with loving arms, looking forward to whatever came next. Compared to all the horrors I've suffered in this hellish plane, the monotony of my life before this seemed like heaven. But my hopes were in vain. I would never be embraced by a beautiful afterlife. I wouldn't even be sent back to the monotony of my old life. To my horror, my body slowly reformed. My organs, my blood, my bones, and my skin all came back until I could eventually stand. I looked at the endless abyss in front of me and began to walk again. A damned soul, doomed to walk, doomed to suffer. Do not take the things you have in vain no matter their monotony, for a damned man, monotony is heaven.

WHEN HEROES FAIL: ELVES

A RHYTHMIC MADNESS OF metal and pain. The clanging of Andros' shackles and the cracking of his pickaxe against the stone walls were all he had. Vibrations are sent up his arm with every strike, making his hands and arms numb. Andros was an Elvin coal miner. He spent eighteen hours of his day mining coal to feed the industrial machine of the Strahdian Empire. *'Clang,'* Another strike with his pickaxe, knocking more pieces of rock from the wall. He breathed heavily, his lungs on fire, his arms numb from hours of swinging, and his legs should've given way long ago. The combination of being overworked and malnourished would have killed him in any other circumstance, yet he kept going, forced by the enchanted necklaces his race was forced to wear. The necklaces kept him and the rest of his kind going, even when their bodies should've collapsed from the strain. This didn't prevent their bodies from taking damage, however. Their skin was still bruised, their muscles still torn, and their bones were still broken. Yet they mined on.

Andros heard a moan a few feet away, one of his kin had collapsed.

"His amulet fell off," another Elf said bleakly. "It must've been knocked off or been snagged by a rock." Without it, all the fatigue from years of work hit the collapsed Elf all at once.

"H-Help me," he begged but no one came to his aid. They were all too afraid.

"What's going on here," an angry voice bellowed out. It was one of the Dark Elves. "Ah, so the traitor thinks he can stop working,"

"No please, I didn't-"

Before he could finish, the Dark Elf drew a barbed whip from his hip. A loud crack could be heard, followed by a scream and the tearing of flesh. The Dark Elf brought the whip down over and over again, seeming to enjoy the pain he caused. He let out a sadistic laugh and kicked the amulet over to the tortured Elf, who was barely moving. "Get back to work traitor. I won't be so merciful next time."

Andros had seen this punishment done to many of his kind. The Elves' once fair and soft skin was cut and gashed open. Their blood spilled onto the floor and over the Dark Elves' armor as the Dark Elves grinned from ear to ear. "Traitors aren't meant to stop. Your eternal lives are meant to be spent fueling our greatness, the greatness you sought to destroy," they would say to the Elves. *"Traitors"* was the name the Dark Elves had given them. Traitors because they had sided with the race of men, the race that had enslaved the Elves thousands of years ago and was responsible for their falling into darkness.

'Crack.' The sound of the whip rang across the entirety of the mine as the Elf next to Andros screamed out in horrid agony. The Elf who had been whipped stopped for a moment to adjust the grip of his pickaxe.

"No stopping, worm," The Dark Elf said to him. "Even those worthless humans lasted longer than you did."

Andros had heard what was happening to the race of man. The human race that had fought with him side by side, their shields next to his, their swords cut down the same enemy. That race was almost completely gone.

Andros continued to slam his pickaxe into the rock, each hit sending powerful vibrations through his hands and up my arms. He felt his body slowly going numb, however, the amulet kept him from stopping. Whenever his arms began to feel weak the amulet would glow a vibrant purple. It made the numbness fade away, though this was no blessing. His body still showed all the damage of being overworked, malnourished, and beaten. The amulet simply allowed his body to work despite the pain, despite his brain begging him to stop. The end had to come to this: his kind never being able to see the sun, never being able to feel the breeze dance through the trees, and it was the worst kind of torture.

Andros looked around. Seeing no guards, he quickly placed his hand on the stone wall of the mine. "Give me something, anything," he quietly pleaded. He reached out with his mind in a vain attempt to feel some sort of life, but he was met with darkness. What are they to do, rot like this for all eternity? Were Elvin's children to never sing again? Are their histories and costumes just supposed to be swept away by the sands of time? Are they to never bask in the light of the sun? They could no longer stand for this. The time had come when they needed to see the sun again.

Andros didn't go back to the mass pits they were made to crawl into to sleep that night. Instead, he waited for someone.

"Andros," someone whispered from around the corner. It was his love Fillebryn. They had known each other for a hundred years (in fact, the next day would be the hundred and first year.) They'd been married 50 of those years.

"Fillebryn," Andros said, bringing him in for an embrace. It had been months since they had seen each other. "Has everything been gathered?" Andros looked him over. He had become dreadfully skinny, his once-toned body now looked like the body of a starved animal. His rib bones were visible due to his lack of body fat.

"Yes, it has. Everything has been prepared for tomorrow and everyone knows the plan." Fillebryn said.

Andros saw the worried look on Fillebryn's face. "What's wrong, Fillebryn?"

"I'm terrified, Andros. Terrified that the plan won't work and that we'll never again feel the sun on our faces, or the grass on our feet. However, the thing that terrifies me most of all is the possibility that I'll never see you again." Tears flowed down Fillebryn's cheeks like the rivers that flowed down the mountains. Andros placed his forehead against Fillebryn's and assured him that they would lay in the sun once again.

The next day, Andros and the rest of the Elves all began work as normal. They were all in on the plan, sharing glances and wondering when it would all start. Hours passed and some began to think that the plan had failed before it even began. But then a steady rumble moved across the mine.

The Dark Elves panicked. "One of the caves must have collapsed," one of them said.

Andros smiled. "No, it's not a collapse," he said to himself "It's the hoards upon hoards of those you have oppressed through the years. It is the wrath of the traitors, the wrath of the Elves."

The rumbles grew louder and louder, screams and roars closer and closer.

The Elves came stained with crimson blood and fire in their eyes. One of Andros' kinsmen brought their pickaxe down into the skull of one of their oppressors, and it exited through the bottom of his jaw. The Dark Elf dropped to his knees before the pickaxe ripped off the front of the Dark Elves' face. The amulets they were forced to wear were now being turned against the Dark Elves. The amulets allowed the Elves to work no matter how sore, tired, or hurt they were. allowed them to fight despite having been starved and overworked.

When the dust cleared from the attack Andros saw that Fillebryn was one of the Elves who had killed their captors. They gave each other a welcoming smile as Fillebryn broke Andro's chains.

"How is everything going so far?" Andros asked.

"So far so good. The Dark Elves were caught by surprise and are completely disorganized. Over the years they have become less alert and have begun to underestimate us." He managed to get the remaining chains off Andros' wrists and feet.

"Good, but we need better equipment. We won't get far if all we have is pickaxes," Andros said, rubbing his wrists. He knelt and began to strip the weapons and usable armor from the dead Dark Elves who lay at their feet.

They distributed what armor and weapons they could get among the small group they had. It was more of a patchwork than an army, but it would do for the time being. Phase two of their plan would soon begin. They needed to link up with the other groups that had successfully broken away from their captors.

When the Elves moved through the tunnels their amount of equipment numbers slowly grew. They felt a ravenous sense of satisfaction at the knives, swords, whips, and other such weapons of torture being used to rid themselves of their captors. Not all groups were as lucky to break free. They saw many of their kind cut down in brutal ways. Some had been killed slowly, some had their bodies violated. This only served to ignite their rage even more. Andros and the rest of the Elf kin were determined to free themselves of such a fate and avenge those who had suffered.

When the Elves linked up with the rest of the survivors, they began their final assault. They quickly moved through the tunnels, blitzing the Dark Elves in small groups. They held nothing back. None of them died quickly from a quick stab. They were torn apart, beaten, and whipped to death.

One of the Dark Elves managed to catch Andros off guard and tackled him to the ground. "Traitorous scum," he screamed. He held a dagger above his head, but a spear went through the back of his skull and out of his mouth before he could stab Andros. Blood and broken teeth splattered onto Andros's face. The Dark Elf coughed as his brain tried to process what had just happened. Andros grabbed the wooden handle of the spear by both ends. He rotated it quickly, breaking The Dark Elf's neck before the abomination fell to the ground.

As the last of the Dark Elves in the group were dealt with, Andros turned to Fillebryn. "You have saved me yet again."

"Don't think about thanking me. You saved me countless times during the war."

Andros smiled at the memories. The smile quickly faded though when he realized that thoughts of war had made him smile. How far had he slipped, how much horror had he gone through that those memories of steel and conquest were now enough to bring him joy simply because he was less hungry and had companions? Tears rolled down his cheeks but he quickly wiped them away when Fillebryn placed a hand on his shoulder and said, "The pain will stop one day."

Before Andros could respond, there was a rumble nearby. Dark Elves. Dozens of them with rage in their eyes appeared. They must have been stationed at the back of the cave. They had managed to organize and were now ready for the Elves. Under any other circumstance, they would have offered the Elves a deal to keep their workforce. 'Stop now and you'll live,' one would expect them to say, but after what the Elves had done, they'd only be satisfied with blood. And that worked for the Elves. There was no deal that the Dark Elves could offer that the

Elves would accept. The Elves would die fighting for their right to lay in the sun again before they went back to work another day in those forsaken mines.

Both sides cried out in battle as they charged at each other. The Dark Elves outnumbered the Elves but in the tight tunnels, their numbers meant nothing. They crashed against each other, steel clashed against steel, shields were shaken, and blood was spilled. As weapons clashed, vibrations were sent through the hands of all, and as the battle dragged on, stamina was drained. In a normal battle, the Elves would have had no chance at victory. But thanks to the amulets, things like hunger and exhaustion did not affect them.

The Elves had them on the run and they were about to kill the rest of their captors, but the cowards were not ready to grant the Elves that satisfaction. As the Dark Elves ran, they began to take out some of the support beams that held up the tunnels. Dirt began to fall on them. The ground rumbled as if one of the ancient beasts had awoken. The Elves abandoned their pursuit and made a break for the only exit they knew to exist. Even though they had been down here for years, they hadn't forgotten the way out.

As the Elves drew near the exit, they began to see the sun. The golden exit glowed warmly in the distance, calling them all to its warm embrace. Andros made sure everyone made it out. As the last one exited the caves, he leaped forward, managing to escape just as the entrance collapsed behind them. "Freedom," he said, collapsing on the soft grass.

Years had been spent without feeling grass. He had almost forgotten how soft it was. He moved his hand gently across it, feeling every single blade that blessed his sense of touch. He took in the aroma of the world around him after years of breathing nothing but dust and the iron smell of blood. To finally have the smell of grass, flowers, and trees flood his nostrils was an immeasurable pleasure. To him and the rest of his kind, this was like being embraced by the heavens.

Fillebryn lay next to him, basking in the sun. The sight almost broke Andros, as it had been so long since he'd seen his love truly happy. He looked so beautiful, with his long, golden hair sparkling in the sunlight. His green eyes highlighted by the natural fauna around them made Andros' heart skip a beat. He'd forgotten that passion. His heart thumped no longer from fear, but from love.

"What happens now?" Fillebryn asked.

Andros quickly realized the struggle wasn't over. What were they to do now? They'll be found if they stayed, and their list of allies was immensely thin. But not all was lost. He knew for a fact they were still alive.

"We find my brother. The half-breed."

WHEN HEROES FAIL: HUMANS

MY NAME IS ZARREN, and my race is slowly fading away. The camps are dark and wet due to the near-constant rain that falls here. This specific camp lies on a coast that was once a grand kingdom serving as a home to millions. It is now a burning wasteland that has the corpses of millions scattered throughout the kingdom. It is the worst in the city of Tog. When you walk there, it isn't rough dirt or soft, fertile grass that was once the home of many flower beds beneath your feet. Instead, it's the rotting bodies of the city's people. The city center is where they stacked the bodies of the children.

The rest of us are crammed into the small barracks that weren't meant to hold a dense population. Five of us have to sleep in a bed meant for one person and that's if we're lucky. The lack of personal space at night is almost a blessing compared to what happens during the day. The labor we are forced to do when the sun rises is meaningless most of the time. We put rocks into a cart only to put them back the next day. The day after that we break them. We store food only to let it spoil, we build more barracks to have them stuffed, or they just make us stay outside. Then we're made to tear down the new barracks because we "didn't do it right." The ones who are forced to stay outside often freeze to death due to the rain. Dying in such a way is considered a blessing here, for there are far worse ways to die.

Sickness spreads quickly and indiscriminately, slowly torturing and killing everyone it encounters. The sickness doesn't start badly. One's muscles start to ache and the body gets so tired that some don't wake up for several days. Then comes the crimson. When one's eyes eventually open, blood will start to pour out of them as if the person were crying rose petals. Blood will then start coming out of every orifice and in much larger quantities than should be possible. The sickness causes the body to speed up its blood production. The blood will then start to come out of the victim's pores. If the victim isn't dead before this point, they are now leaking contagious blood that will spread to others. This plague isn't some long-existing blight on the world, and it isn't an invisible terror that has been killing for a millennium. It's new, and it was made by the Dark Elves.

They come in the night, with their skin as dark as the night sky and their eyes either glowing a deep shade of purple or a blood-red crimson. They come, and when we wake up in the morning at least one of us is missing, taken to their rooms to be experimented on. Elves are naturally curious people, you see. They love to learn, figure things out, and make new things. Dark Elves are the same way, yet due to the corruption and hatred over what happened to them thousands of years ago, they have twisted and bastardized that curiosity into something wicked and cruel.

Sometimes they'll make several small cuts on a person. They never go too deep because they know that a person could die of blood loss and they would rather have them suffer in other ways. They want to see if the person will die from the sheer pain of being cut hundreds, if not thousands, of times. Why would they want to know this? The human race is known for its iron will and the ability to face almost any hardship together. They are curious to see how far that iron will stretch.

When we arrived here, the Dark Elves gave a few of us a drink. We all thought it was water. Now we know differently. In that drink was a sickness that made us unable to have children. They are thorough in our extinction. This way, even if some of us managed to escape, we would have no way to continue our bloodlines and our mortal lives would eventually cause us to fade away, whether they recaptured us or not.

It may take years or even decades to kill us all, but if there is one thing the Dark Elves have its time. With their immortal lives, they will gladly spend all those years tracking down and killing each one of us and making sure all of our histories are erased. I sometimes wonder why they didn't make us all drink it. I can only assume they only wanted to test it. Maybe they didn't know if it would work, or they simply didn't have enough. I try not to think of such things, but when faced with such horrors, my mind starts to lose its grip and begins to wonder.

We had another death march today, another one of their grizzly experiments. They take us out for walks, walks that span miles, with no footwear or clothes of any kind. This is to see how long a body can go on without rest. They'll walk us for days at a time in some cases. In other cases, they'll fire an arrow into a person's leg, or cut their legs with a dagger and then force them to walk to see how long a person can walk with injuries. Some collapse from exhaustion, and those who do are instantly fired upon by arrows. The results are written down, and their bodies are fed to the large beasts that they ride; beasts that stand taller than any man, whose fur is as dark as their Elvin masters, and whose eyes are filled with nothing but hatred for anything that it views as inferior. Its teeth are sharper than daggers and its hulking body could take down a bear as if it were a grown man pinning down a child.

The march has made many unable to walk or stand for several days, their feet cut and infected from the torture. Many of those who do survive the walks wind up killing themselves. They know if they live they'll have to walk again.

All that we're subjected to tortures to our minds, as well. Many screams throughout the night and many are just frozen with fear. People have clawed and bitten off their flesh, ripped out their own eyes, or they just decided to end it all. The Dark Elves revel in this, of course. They find it so satisfying that we, humans, finally get what we deserve. Punishment for something that happened thousands of years ago.

Even after all I've been through, however, I still don't know everything the Dark Elves do to us or the reason for all of their experiments. I've seen completely skinned bodies, and people combined either with magic or with a needle and thread. I've seen twins disappear but when one returns with the attributes of both. People have come back with their eyes missing, or limbs that didn't origi-nally belong to them. These are just a few of the things I've seen but I doubt I'll see much more. Unlike the Elves made to gather materials, or the Dwarves who are forced to make weapons and machines responsible for the slaughter of millions, I am meant to die.

However, the thing about humans is that we are a stubborn race, and nothing unites us more than a common enemy. Humans from all across the world were here, from all walks of life and many different kingdoms. From the deserts to the cold mountains of the north, (the ladder is where I'm from) we all had one common goal: to get out of this Godforsaken place and return to our lives as free men and women.

Many of us were former warriors. Being part of *The Band of Heros,* I took the lead in planning. I remember those days as if they were yesterday: the dwarf who was the only one who could outdrink me and the elf who had a fondness for the sun and nature. He and I got along surprisingly well once we got to know each other. We both loved nature, especially birds. His brother the half breed, (half Northman, half-Elf) was the best of us. Without him, we wouldn't have gotten as far as we did. I don't know where he is, but I know in my heart he is still alive.

We finalized the plan that one night. There was a bridge that the Dark Elves used to carry supplies into the compound. The whole place was surrounded by a dugout pit filled with wooden spikes so the bridge was the only way in or out. And we would have to cross it.

"Are you mad?" one of the others chimed in as I explained the plan. "We plan to leave through the front gate?"

"It is our only option," I said. "If we tried to dig out we would eventually reach the pit and either die or be stuck. If we go over the walls then we would fall right into them. Any other plan is suicide."

"And this plan isn't? This plan requires us to fight them. You want people who have hardly eaten, who are sick and dying, to fight against highly trained and armored Dark Elves who currently outmatch us in every way?"

I could tell that his words got to the rest of them. They had doubt painted all over their pale, sickly faces. "We have no other choice," I said. "But there is one thing that could give us an advantage."

"What would that be?" one of the others said, a hopeful gleam in his eye.

I gave a small smile, "The Hallbane."

The other Northmen and those of the men from other kingdoms who recognized the name looked surprised or simply smiled. Others had a look of confusion.

"To those who do not know, The Hallbane is an herb that certain Northmen warriors use. On its own, it's not much, but when it's ground up into a powder and inhaled..." The memories from my past experiences with the herb flooded in; being able to pick up full-grown men with one arm, cleaving through a fully armored warrior with one swing, and crushing someone's skull with nothing but my hands.

"It does what?" one of the men asked,

"It gives you a small taste of the power that a God holds," I said grinning.

"A good plan," one of my fellow Northmen said. "But how do we get a hold of it? We can't expect it to grow here. There is far too much rain even if we did have the seeds, and there is no way for us to get wild ones."

"Don't forget Captain Balsar," another man said. Balsar was the Dark Elf captain who was by far the cruelest person and the deadliest warrior. He made a personal appearance at every execution, even doing trial by combat just so he could kill someone himself.

Both men had a point. There was far too much rain to grow anything in the compound, let alone the Hellbane. Not to mention that if Balsar caught us, none of us would stand a chance without the Hellbane. Thankfully, neither of these facts would be an issue.

"The Dark Elves have been bringing it into the compound since we got here," I said. "They've been running their experiments on it. They want to know how it works and what effects it has on other races or animals, no doubt to try and improve their armies. We just have to take it ourselves. As for Balsar, he'll be gone tomorrow. I heard him say that he's being given some award for his great service." Light laughter moved throughout the crowd and I saw a wave of hope wash through the eyes of everyone for the first time in what seemed like an eternity.

"We might not be able to get enough Hellbane for everyone." one of the men said.

"We won't need enough for everyone. With Hellbane, a few good warriors can take down an army," I told him.

"When do we start?" asked another.

"A fresh batch of Hellbane comes tomorrow," I said, unable to hide my excitement. "Those Dark Elves sure are efficient, huh?"

That night as everyone lay in their beds, I prayed to my Gods for the first time since we lost the war. "I have no offering to give, nothing to give in return, all I can do is ask you for two things." I looked up to the rotten wooden ceiling of the hut I slept in "The first thing is to please stop the rain tomorrow just for a few hours or at least a few minutes. It would greatly improve our odds. The second is that I want you to give the rest of the people here your favor and have them make it out of this. If I am to live, that is good, but if my death would save others then I do not oppose it. For I know I am destined for your halls in the next life, and I would have the satisfaction of knowing that the cost of my life saved countless others."

I let out a deep breath, now visible in the cold air, and looked up through a small hole in the roof. There was a small hole in the rain clouds and I could see the shining moon perfectly. It was full and it radiated a light that I had not seen in so long. Tears slid down my cheeks in a sense of pure joy and happiness. The gods were listening, and I knew that they had listened well for they were already starting to grant one of my requests.

Morning broke and our plan was put into motion, but first the distraction. As we left our huts, we acted like we were starting a riot. People yelled out protests, fake fights broke out between us, and insults were thrown. A small group of us went to the door where they took us when they dragged us away to be experimented on. Usually, the door was heavily guarded, but since the distraction called for more guards to come and try to quell it, now there were only two. My group nodded to me before they rushed one of the guards, knocking him to the ground before he could draw his weapon. The other guard came to help but I quickly slammed him into the stone wall before grabbing his head and quickly snapping his neck, his lifeless body dropping to the ground. I saw that the others had beaten the other guard to death or into a coma. It didn't matter as long as they wouldn't be an issue. Thankfully, many of the others had given me their share of their food the previous night, which made doing what I just did that much easier. They said that my strength mattered the most so even though I protested, they gave me their food.

I found the keys to the door of the Dark Elf I had killed and used them to open the door. We hid the bodies beneath one of the floorboards in the huts and checked to see if anyone had heard us. Luckily, due to the noise of the staged riot, it appeared that no one had heard a thing. We went through the heavy metal door and the smell hit us like a wave crashing against the shore. The smell of rotten meat, death, and decay was so thick that some of the people with me immediately doubled over losing what little food they had eaten. The smell was even worse than the huts but we forced ourselves to keep going.

We didn't have long to pull this off. Sooner or later the commotion outside would either be quelled or escalate to the point of retaliation, and we couldn't have that happen. As we moved through the long, cold, stink-filled hallway we saw several rooms that all had different labels on the doors. The labels were all written in Dark Elvish speech, but the Half Breed and his brother had taught me Elvish, and the Dark Elvin variant wasn't too different so I was able to make out the words. I wished I hadn't been able.

The rooms were labeled 'The Cooler', 'Surgical', and 'Harvester'. By far the most ominous and the one that sent the coldest chill down my spine was the room that was simply labeled 'Food.' So many questions circled through my head. Food for what? Them? Their beasts? I froze at my next thought. Us? My blood turned to ice when I realized that this was the room where that horrid smell was emanating from. I reached out to open the door and just as my hand felt the cold metal frame my comrades called for me, saying they had found the Hellbane.

I took one last glance at the room before walking over to them. Sure enough, the door in front of us was labeled 'Hellbane'. We used the key on the door, but it didn't open.

"What do we do now?" one of the men asked as he looked around to see if anyone was coming. "We'll have to force it open. With all of us slamming into it we might be able to knock it over."

"Are you mad? They'll hear us for sure!" they yelled.

"We have no other choice. We have no time to look for the key and every second we waste brings the plan closer and closer to failure," I said.

One of them let out a groan. "These herbs better work as well as you say they will."

We threw our bodies against the large metal door. The loud metallic clang echoed through the long hallway, but the door stood unbroken.

"Dragons balls, how strong is the steel?"

I gritted my teeth. "Quit complaining and keep going." We slammed our bodies into the door again, this time the door dented slightly.

"I think my shoulder is giving out," one of the men said.

I felt my weakened body protesting what I was doing. "Once we have the herbs you won't feel the pain anymore, just keep going," I said. Voices off in the distance slowly got closer.

We slammed into the door again. This time the door bent as one of its hinges broke loose. I quickly broke off the other hinge, the metal door warping and hitting the ground with a loud crash. I could hear voices yelling when they caught onto what was going on. The Dark Elves were getting closer. We ran into the room and found the herbs, the footsteps getting closer and closer. They would surely execute many of us after discovering the plan.

We grabbed the herbs and could hear what the Dark Elves were saying. Slurs and orders cut through the air like blades. We brought the herbs up to our faces and inhaled as the Dark Elves entered.

We were all relaxing in our barracks. Our duties had just ended and the other soldiers had taken our place. Right after the prisoners began to riot, my duties were done for the day so it was no longer my problem. I didn't understand why we kept them around anyway. They were more trouble than they were worth and if you ask me, we should have just executed them all to be done with them. I slipped off my plated armor shoes and lay back on the bed, thinking of home.

Beautiful architecture and lights shine at night, making it seem like the stars have come down to light the city. Now that we had taken our old land back from our traitorous kind, we could repopulate those areas and make them shine like the full moon in the night sky. I hadn't been to *The Emerald Forest* in a thousand years since I and the rest of my kind split off. I heard that our forces had burned it down, but that couldn't be true. I think we claimed to have done that as a way of demoralizing the enemy forces. There's no way our forces would burn down our old homes.

As I pondered this, a loud, metallic crash came from down the hallway. We all shot up from our beds and looked at each other wondering what was going on. We got off our beds and rushed toward the noise. It was most likely just one of our beasts getting reckless, but even so, it would need to be taken care of quickly so it didn't break its containment. Another loud metallic bang but this time it was accompanied by human voices. We ran as we realized that humans had broken into the secret areas.

"Quickly, don't let them into the research rooms!" I said to my fellow soldiers as we rushed to the source of the noise.

There was another bang and the sound of a metal door breaking and smashing onto the hard floor.

"Stop, man filth," one of the soldiers yelled out as we approached.

"You're dead, you slavers!" I said. What I saw next sent a cold shiver down my spine. The label on the broken door said 'Hellbane'. As I read those words

I remembered the monstrous Northmen that I had fought during the war who used the Hellbane herb. It turned normal men into crazed warriors, and it turned hardened warriors into monsters who fought like rabid bears. These former prisoners were the latter.

As soon as one of them saw us, she rushed over with the speed of a crazed bear and slammed the soldier to my right so hard into the wall that they broke through the stone wall and slammed into the next wall. The crazed warrior woman looked at me with blood-red eyes. It was clear I was next. She took a swipe at me. I couldn't doge and the blow collided with my torso. I felt the armor bend and warp against my body before my ribs cracked and broke as easily as rotten wood.

I slammed into the wall next to the corpse of my fallen comrade, my insides burning with pain. My lungs tried to take in air but couldn't. They had been stabbed by my broken ribs. The monsters made quick work of the rest of the soldiers that were with me. It was clear that we would never see the lights of our cities again when the leader of the men walked over to me. He was bigger than the others, a hulking man who hailed from the northern kingdoms of men. What scum, I thought, hoping that when all is said and done, the men from the north are the first to go. I gave one last spit of blood that landed on his foot. He then took that foot and crushed my skull with it.

The herbs made us feel like Gods. Raw power seemed to flow through our veins like blood. We roared like beasts as we killed the Dark Elves that had tried to stop us. We rushed out of the building as our rage-filled bodies demanded vengeance and blood. We broke through the wall and saw the panic in the eyes of all the Dark Elves as well as some of our own as they wondered if we would turn on them. Even though our minds were filled with rage, we could still tell friends from foes. We rushed the Dark Elves that were in the courtyard of the prison. Arrows pierced our skin, and some Dark Elves managed to slash at us with swords, but because of the Hellbane, we hardly felt any pain and we weren't slowed down at all.

We ripped them apart in such a brutal fashion that even an experienced warrior would lose the contents of his stomach. However, our enemy wasn't going to go down without a fight.

Four of them surrounded me. One took a slash at me but I caught his arm, snapping it before taking his sword and stabbing him. While I was distracted by him one of the others shot an arrow through my shoulder. I let out a roar and went after him but then an axe hit my back. Luckily, the increased muscle that the herb granted stopped it from causing too much damage. I turned around and punched him in the stomach, sending him flying and causing him to let go of his axe. I grabbed it and stopped the blow of the fourth Dark Elf who had a sword. As I blocked this attack, fear filled his eyes when he realized he had just seconds to live. I knocked the sword out of his hand and swung the axe as hard as I could, cleaving him in half. The archer readied another arrow but I quickly held up the severed torso of the Elf as a shield.

Panic overtook him as he drew another arrow but his normally refined fingers fumbled and dropped the arrow. He quickly bent down to grab it but I was in front of him and struck his skull as hard as lightning strikes the Earth. The body of the Dark Elf had now been split in two, his organs and blood spread across the stone floor as if it were some morbid painting. I rushed over to the Dark Elf I had sent flying. As I approached his broken body, he pulled out a dagger and tried to catch me off guard, but I caught the blade in my hand. With my blood dripping down the blade, I then snapped the blade off the hilt and shoved it into his neck. He gagged on his blood before I grabbed his head and snapped his neck. His body flopped to the ground.

We were overwhelming their forces, but I knew we wouldn't be able to keep this up forever. Those who had not taken the herbs stood no chance on their own. We had to get out of there right then if we wanted to get out alive.

I called for one of our men to pull the lever that controlled the gate. He quickly ran over to it, throwing one of the Dark Elves over the wall as he went. He cranked the lever, causing the gate to slowly rise, and reveal our freedom.

For the first time in years, I saw the world outside of the camp. It was still as wet as everything inside but simply seeing life and a world that was more than stone and death sent a new kind of happiness through my body. I didn't have much time to admire it. I knew that the Dark Elves who patrolled the lower levels of the camp would soon be upon us.

We all ran when the Dark Elves came up the stairs. As we crossed the bridge I realized that there was no way for us to close the gate. Due to most of our conditions, they would be able to catch up to us instantly. When I realized this I stopped running "Go," was all I said to the rest of my kind. For all, I knew I had seen the last of my entire race, and I couldn't think of a better group of people to start our race anew. What used to be a thought that I would ponder was now our blessing. Those who didn't drink the liquid which made us infertile now held the key to our future.

A few cried, a few protested, and a few ran, but all knew someone had to hold them off, and I was the one who would be able to buy them the most time. The others who had taken the herbs would be needed to help guide and carry some of the others who did not have the strength to do it themselves. As they left, I took a deep breath, clenched my axe, and stood on the bridge alone. They all roared when they charged but my scream drowned them out as I prepared to soon see my fallen comrades.

A Dark Elvin captain, with skin as black as charcoal and eyes as red as fire, looked around the destroyed grounds. He simply couldn't believe what he saw. Around him lay the bodies of over one hundred of their warriors and in front of the other end of the bridge lay the body of one dead human.

"Explain this to me," he commanded one of the surviving soldiers.

"A group of prisoners into the room where we held the herb Hellbane. The effects of the herb are known to turn people into a one-man army, but he was beyond that. It was as if we were fighting a God." The soldier had a look of pure fear in his purple eyes.

The captain growled in frustration as he walked over to the waste of existence that was the dead man and placed a foot on his head. "He is no God, no warrior. He is a starved weakling whose race is on the brink of extinction. You called me here to tell me ghost stories and legends from the war that I have never seen in my hundreds of years of existence. You all will clean every drop of blood from this compound and then you will find and kill all of those who escaped."

The captain tried to move his foot off of the human's head and walk back to his men, but could not. His foot was stuck. Had he caved in the human's skull? No, the man hadn't been dead very long and he hadn't stepped very hard. The Captain looked down. The dead human's hand had grabbed onto his leg.

WHEN HEROES FAIL: DWARVES

I SLAMMED MY HAMMER onto a piece of hot metal. *"Clang"* Another time it would be music to me ears, however, the song playing today was for that old death and destruction. I stepped back and started looking at my horrid creation. It was a massive ship, and not any ol' ship, no, this one could use hot air to fly.

In another life, I would be proud, but I knew what she would be used for. Archers could sit in her and rain arrows of steel, fire, poison, and whatever else they planned. It could also carry oil in large buckets on its sides, which could then be lit to rain fire on entire towns. Millions would burn at my hands. The fire would spread to anyone it touched – man, woman, child, pet, soldier, or innocent. I have fallen so far. I once made grand jewelry for the most lavish Elves, grand buildings that people could use as a home, a shop, or an inn. I remember a time when my name was sung in the great underground halls of my people. "Hernoc The Great Builder," they would cheer. "May his life be as grand and beautiful as his a great many works! May his life last as long as these stone halls, may his eyes for wondrous ores remain as sharp as my axe, and may the dragons tremble when they see the glimmer of his axe."

"May yer nose remains as brown as the trees," someone would chime in whenever someone offered too many compliments. We'd all laugh our asses off and take a swig of our drinks as we enjoyed our lives together. Those times are gone now. They stopped as soon as the Goblin and Orc hordes overran our halls and tore down the walls. I guess one of their wishes came true. I lasted longer than those walls, but I wish every day that I had fallen with them for my life has been spent murdering thousands.

I wish my life had ended in the days that have long since passed. You see, in those days, the Dwarves and Elves were friends. The Elves loved having beautiful clothes, jewelry made from precious materials, lavish homes, and many more beautiful things. We, Dwarves, were experts in making these things, so a long, glorious friendship formed. We taught them the ways of the forge and we worked on many things together. The Great Ships of Agon could fit hundreds of people and were named the Grand Shire of Althos and Gunder, after the first Elf and Dwarf to ever meet. These two monuments, as well as all our other great works, have been torn down to rubble. The world will never again know the things we've created or the alliances we formed. All they'll know is the destruction our forced creations caused and that we are meant to serve the empire.

Our kingdoms fell one by one to the green hoards of the Orcs and Goblins. It wasn't that hard to get the two races to work together. The Goblins love to treasure shiny things and Dwarves had an abundance of these. The Orcs usually lived in tribes in the wilderness and they hated it. They wanted grand fortresses and big halls. Of course, we had these things as well. The Goblins came in uncountable numbers. At first, we managed to hold them back, but after years of fighting and being outnumbered in nearly every battle, each fortress was slowly overrun. Most of our people were slaughtered. The Goblins would swarm a dwarf and stab them again and again until they finally died Orcs would at least kill you outright. They are a tribal race, but they followed a warrior's path.

The worst fate was being killed by an Ogre, a mindless, ugly creature around twelve to fifteen feet tall. They could crush you with their massive feet, destroy your body with a swing of their massive clubs, grab you in their clammy hands and crush you, or use their massive maws filled with teeth as big as a human's forearm to eat you alive. The last thing you would see is your blood and guts falling out, or your being chewed on by the creature in front of you. They'll snap your bones so they can lick the meat off, and bite off your head because they like the taste of your brains. I saw this happen to every one of my comrades in arms, as well as my wife

My wife, my eternal battle maiden, my everything. I had almost forgotten she existed. I've lost track of how many years it's been since I've seen her, as I've been down here since we lost the war...When was that again? My memory has been fading over the years. The Elves keep me working on their machines until it's all I'll know. That's what they intend to do to all the dwarves, work us until we either die or forget everything about our culture, our history, and everything else we once were. The Empire wants to use us as a workforce, building their machines and weapons, forcing us to mate so the next generation will be born into the workforce and know nothing else outside of it. My wife would have rather died than be part of that fate, so that's what she did. She took out as many as she could before eventually falling in battle, her axe laying on her chest. If I forget everything about her, I hope I can at least remember the day that I met her. No matter what they do, I won't let them take the memory away from me.

I wish I could be sent to the mines. That would possibly save my memories. But that's why they have the Elves doing the mining. They know that we Dwarves love the caves, the thrill of finding the shining ores and thinking of the possibilities of it. It's ingrained in us you see, and that's what they fear. They know it could spark a fire in us that would never be extinguished. If we had access to the mines, we could feel like Dwarves again. We'd make our equipment and be able to build a great underground hall. With this we would be able to launch a rebellion, but would we be able to win such a fight? No, but The Empire would lose a key force, our expert craftsmanship, which is something they would rather not lose.

This is why they keep us only working on the crafts. Dwarves love to create as well, but not like this. These are materials mined off the blood of our greatest comrades. The thought of me dying of old age, only for my friends to live on enterally in the mines, fills me with dread. The fact that I am making such crude weapons and machines only meant to kill and destroy adds to the amount of my pain. We Dwarves are prideful in our work. When we make things that we can be proud of, it fills us with joy. But here we are making things out of materials that we did not get ourselves. We are making crude devices made for suffering. There is no beauty in the work we do. That is why it affects us so. We have no pride or joy in what we are doing. This demoralizing work slowly drains us day by grueling day. When we made lavish works for the Elves we felt pride because we saw them enjoying it so much. When we made sharp weapons that did their jobs and cleaved through our enemies we felt joy because we had made weapons that were able to defend our people. When we made our great fortresses we felt pride at the sight of walls that stood as tall as mountains and halls that looked like they were crafted for the Gods themselves. We knew that we did this with our own hands, with the materials we mined ourselves. But now those days are gone, and we will never see them again. My hands will never again touch a pickaxe. I will never swing an axe that is sharper than a Dragon's tooth. All my hands will feel is the cold steel of the Empire's crude weapons, the lifeless ores that are stained with the blood of Elves, and the hot furnaces which smell of burning flesh. Perhaps that's what they did with those human captives I saw. I guess they figured they'd skip the camps and send them straight to their deaths. My comrades mine the bloodstained ores and then provide fuel for the furnace that melts them so I may mold them.

"Oi! Stop your daydreaming Dwarf!" the Orc Boss yelled as I slammed my hammer down on the hot metal. "I don't see why we keep you, Dwarves, around. We Orcs make better weapons anyway." The Orc held up his crude sword. It had a jagged edge like a saw blade and showed light signs of rust. I held back the urge to roll my eyes at his poor excuse for craftsmanship. The sword would suffice if it was meant to torture an unarmored person, or as an intimidation tactic to use on an inexperienced warrior. However, to an experienced warrior who knew what they were doing, it would be a weakness to exploit.

"I suppose it ain't a bad job watchin' you Dwarves. It's its reward for helping those Dark Elves takin' you lot down. Besides, yer kin is the most fun ta play with. The Elves don't scream enough, and the humies die too fast, but you lot are tough. You last oh so long and hardly ever keel over for pain alone." The Orc chuckled as he looked at his sword and then pressed it against my cheek. "You can smell it, can't you? The blood of your fellow kin has stained this blade." He smirked. "Oh, how they screamed as I sawed them in half. None of the warriors begged though." He placed his hand on the table to get leverage as the blade made a small cut on my cheek. The ringing of my hammer hitting the metal seemed to get so loud that it should've defended me. "Your children on the other hand, oh ho how they begged. They screamed for their mothers and fathers, begging and screaming for us to stop as I ripped them open and fed what was left of them to the Goblins." My hammer slammed down once again, but this time it wasn't steel against steel, it was steel against flesh. My hammer, my flawless, heavy, Dwarven-crafted steel hammer collided with his green flesh. When he cried out in pain I felt something, I hadn't felt in a long time. The will and urge to kick some Orc arse.

"You scum I'll--"

Before the filthy Orc could speak anymore I slammed the hammer against his jaw, causing teeth and blood to splatter onto the floor. The Orc held his broken jaw but before he could do anything I slammed my steel hammer down onto his skull. His skull cracked more and more each time I brought my hammer down. Over and over, I slammed it into his skull, roaring louder and louder each time. It felt like all Dwarves were watching as images of my comrades in arms, the family that I'd lost, and my wife, all flashed in my mind. I kept slamming my hammer onto his head until I was hitting nothing but bloody mush.

I stumbled back, my face, hands, and beard all covered in his filthy blood. However, I reveled in the feeling of killing him brought me. Each drop of blood that coated me was revenge for each of my comrades who had fallen. Not just my fellow Dwarves, but all the Elves and Humans that had fallen by my side as well. I will honor the deaths of all the races who have fallen from the dark hordes of that bastard who calls himself a king of the oppressed. A devilish grin spread across my face as I took up my hammer once again. It was time to bring down this forge.

I began to shovel much more coal into the furnace than I was supposed to, causing it to overheat. I saw the bodies of the Humans in there now. They looked as if they were reaching out for something. I studied the corpse of the Orc that I had killed before I hurled it into the fire. The arms of the Humans seemed to hold the body now as it burned in the inferno. "Go in peace, my friends. May that bastard suffer twice as much as you suffered in the next life."

The furnace began to rumble. Bolts and metal began to fall off of it. I ran out of the room when rumbling thunder came from behind me. Orcs and Goblins were frantically yelling as they tried to figure out what was happening. I ran down a dark hallway to another door and kicked it open. The door led to the outside.

I hadn't seen the outside world in years and now I wish I hadn't. Machines making a constant stream of weapons and armor littered the ground, and they pumped black smoke into the air as they did so. The air was hot and dry, only providing my lungs with slight relief from the air I had been breathing inside the tower. This land was a forest once. It was called "The Emerald Relm" on account of its lush and lively wildlife, and it was home to the Emerald Elves. Knowing them, they made these bastards pay for every tree they burned down, which gave some purpose to their extinction at least.

I didn't have much time to ponder this, however. Goblins came through a door a floor below me, "Up there!" one of them called out. They let out low, disgusting growls as they ran to me.

I didn't run or try to hide, I was done with that. All I did was ready my hammer. Due to the narrowness of the staircase, they could only come at me one at a time, and one Goblin was no match for a rampaging Dwarf. Before the first one could even take a swipe at me I swung my hammer at its head, sending it falling off the staircase to the apocalyptic hellscape below. The second Goblin rushed me and took a swipe at me with its short sword, but I managed to dodge it and counter with an upward swing that connected to his chin. This swing stunned him, allowing me a second swing. This time downwards, the swing crushed his brain.

I quickly grabbed its short sword. "Normally I wouldn't be caught dead using a Goblin weapon," I said and quickly threw it at the third Goblin. It straight through its throat. "But I'll give you special treatment after your generous hospitality."

"How dare you!" one of the Goblins yelled. He shot an arrow that hit my shoulder. I grit my teeth and charged him before he could read a second arrow. I swung my hammer hard enough to knock the Goblin's head clean off. The last

Goblin was shaking in fear at what he'd seen. I looked into his dark eyes, and even though I saw no color in them, I saw that they were the eyes of a coward. He probably took this job assuming he'd get to mess around with weak prisoners who couldn't fight back. This was likely his first fight and it would be his last.

He made a desperate charge at me but I caught his wrist with my hand. Goblins are about the same size as Dwarves, but they don't come close to having our strength. I bent his arm at a downward angle, causing his bone to break through his yellowish-green skin. He let out a scream before I pushed the arm up. The exposed bone went through his head, causing him to drop dead.

I slumped onto the ground, panting hard as my lungs tried to take in what little air was left in this place. I tried to move my arm, but I could only move from the elbow down. Not the shoulder. I knew the arrow was most likely poisoned. Goblins are aresholes like that and I knew the poison would probably eventually kill me. I looked to the red and black sky as the wind flowed through my long hair and beard. "Don't worry about my love. I'll be home soon."

Hammer in hand, I caught my breath and made my way to the door that the Goblins had come through. It led to a long winding staircase. As I went down the stairs a loud rumble shook the entire tower. A loud groaning sound preceded a large crash that erupted from the bottom of the tower. I guessed it was the furnace exploding and the top of the tower falling to the ground. I smiled as all my work and plans were up there, but the task wasn't done. There was a grand furnace at the bottom of the tower for larger pieces of metal. It had to go, and when it did it, would take the rest of the tower down with it.

I ran as quickly down the stairs as I could. Goblins tried to stop me, but each one met a brutal end at the hands of my hammer. One tried to tackle me, but I did a short uppercut with my bad arm and caught him off guard, allowing me to smash him into the ground with my hammer. He was the last one before I reached the grand boiler, but my heart sank slightly when I saw that it wasn't lit. I'd have to do this myself. Lucky for me, the whole place was in chaos. Most of the forces in or around the tower were either dead or fleeing for their lives. I quickly began to shovel coal and wood into the huge furnace then I dumped oil into it. The oil was not only used to fuel this furnace but was eventually going to be loaded up and transported to be used to burn what little forces stood against the Empire. It was good that this would no longer happen.

I was about to light it when the ground erupted behind me, causing most of the floor to crumble and knock me over. A large, black arm erupted from the rubble, slowly revealing an Ogre. Its eyes glowed as it roared and charged me. I tried to get to the furnace, but the Ogre grabbed me in its huge hands. One of my arms was free, so I brought my hammer down on its finger, breaking it and causing the Ogre to let out a roar of pain. It dropped me, and I landed on my back, causing the air in my lungs to leave me. I forced myself to crawl forward to light the furnace again but the bastard kicked me. I flew into the wall and felt several of my bones crack.

I looked through the small hole in the wall and saw several towers like the one I was in. I hadn't seen them before because this must've been the furthest tower and it faced the cliff. I felt my will break slightly as the monstrous Ogre placed its foot on me.

It all seemed pointless now. No matter what I did it would not have mattered, would it? I failed everyone I've ever known and no matter what I could have done nothing would have changed that. Is that what I'm supposed to believe? Well, fuck that. I was taking this tower and this big bastard down. Who cares if I couldn't take them all? Who cares if this was just one tower among many? I will make the bastards know that they aren't invincible, that they can fall, and I will bring honor to all that I used to know.

I pulled the arrow from my shoulder and stabbed the leg of the ugly creature, causing it to stagger. This allowed me to slam my hammer with all the strength I had left into its ankle. This broke the bone and the creature fell. I grabbed the fallen torch and threw it into the furnace. Once again, I saw the faces of all who had been with me: my wife, the Elf, the Human that fought with me, and all the others that died along the way. They held me close and warmed me. But one face wasn't there. The Half Breed.

THE SERVUS

"MY COUNTRY IS DIVINE and just. My country is a master craftsman and I am its humble tool. My country is right." I said this first thing in the morning just as I did any other day, just as any other good citizen started the day. I then looked over at the picture on the wall of our leader and bowed to it proudly. The poster was of a tall, strong man with blue eyes that were as blue as the sea. ("The Appendix of Basic Knowledge" that was given to all citizens said that the sea is blue even though the servus had never personally seen it with their own eyes.)

I changed out of my sleep clothes and into my work clothes. Sleep clothes consisted of a basic shirt and pants that were colored red so they would be easier to see in the dark should they be spotted not sleeping. Work clothes consisted of a heavier gray shirt that had an occupation printed on the front and back, and orange pants and paper-like shoes. Today would be a busy day at my job as there was to be an execution of today's traitors and the leaders of our government always liked their frozen, milky treats on these days. My job is to make these cold treats for the leaders of our government. I didn't have complete knowledge of what they were or why the leaders of our government enjoyed them so much, but it didn't matter. It pleased them and that was the best a citizen could do.

I walked down the street that I walked every morning on my way to work, but something was different, a new building had been destroyed. The rubble of the once-tall building was now a pile of metal and brick on the ground. Bombings by enemy machines that flew through the air were common, but seeing as there was only one building destroyed, I assumed that it was an attack done by one person, and the conversations of nearby people seemed to agree with that statement. As we cleared away, two members of the education department walked up to a small wall of bricks that had managed to stay up despite the destruction of the building and hung a poster of our leader. At least the building still had a purpose now, but that did not stop the rage that flowed through me.

Filth, that's all people like that were. Filth like that only serves to get in the way of our country's glorious progress and seek to undo all that has been accomplished. I hope that with all my being that the man will be executed today.

I eventually reached my job location and readied myself for my duties, making sure all the ingredients were ready and the machines worked properly. (This man doesn't list it here but the workplace for his occupation was a small, gray metal box with a machine inside to dispense the treats and a screen that displays the flavor the customer wanted. They also weren't allowed to talk to the leaders or even see them, so they sat in complete silence in dim light. There was also a small container in the room that would hold the cups that the frozen milk would be held in, as well as a chair for them to sit in. That was it, "It was all a citizen needed.")

I stretched before I sat down, the chair squeaking slightly as the legs of the chair ground against the metal. I flipped the switch that showed I was ready to take the orders and then they started. White, brown, pink, the orders came one by one. I filled the cups with the color of treat they wanted and pushed them out the small window. I never see which leaders like which flavor as is the law. My *"Rules of the Dominus"* book said that we the Servus are never meant to see the Dominus. I agreed with this, of course, for we were simply the workers of the country and not worthy to see people so glorious as the leaders of our nation. (Note that the Dominus were the higher-ups of the country. Also, note that the common people didn't know what the words "servus" and "dominus" meant.)

The orders continued. As each one came and went, I got more and more excited each time as I knew it meant that the execution of the criminals came closer and closer. I knew it would be the man who had destroyed the building in the night as criminals could never hide for long. Our government was everywhere. It was a part of our lives and integrated perfectly. They could never hide for more than a day or so. Finally, the last item on the board came and went, and I gleefully left my workroom and back into the street.

As soon as I left the room, I could hear the roar of the gathered crowd. Everyone was screaming and yelling hateful things at those who were to be executed as we always did when an execution happened. It is patriotic to do so as we are all perfect Servus of the country. Five people were brought out onto the execution stage, causing the rest of the crowd and I to erupt even louder with our rage and hate. I was close enough to study the faces of the filth on the stage. One was a tall man with a dirty face and brown hair who had no expression on his face. The next two were twin females who looked void of emotion as if they couldn't process what was going on, and the short man that stood next to them looked the same. The last one, however, was strange. The first man looked as if he simply knew what he did and had no regrets, the next three simply were void, but the fifth man was cryi ng.

He was crying heavily, streams of tears flowing down his cheeks and dripping onto the stage. This only served to make us angrier but before we all got too rowdy, a large microphone began to rise from the ground behind the stage. We all began to quiet down as we knew what this meant. The head leader of our nation was about to speak.

The voice came, it was powerful and stoic booming with sheer strength, "My loyal Servorum before you today stand the five people who destroyed the three buildings in your great city this morning."

I must have misremembered, but now that I think about it, I'm sure I saw three destroyed buildings today and the people at the wreckage said five people were responsible.

"Today we seek to punish those who seek to destroy and oppress us. These so-called men and women sided with our great enemies who nearly brought us to ruin, but they could not hide. These pathetic excuses of people couldn't hide from us for even a day before our great eyes were able to seek them out."

We all looked proudly at the microphone as the words of our leader filled us with pride. His words were true. These were not men and women in front of us, but simply filth that is no better than a pile of meat who had gained the ability to speak.

"These agents of terror who are the source of all your hardships and fears will meet justice here today!" he said with a thunderous voice as we all let out cheers and applause. With the death of these five pieces of meat, we would be that much closer to making our lives perfect.

The prisoners were asked if they had any last words. The first man simply spat on the ground, the two twins and the fourth man stayed silent as if their brains had simply given up on trying to figure out what was going on, and the fourth man who had been crying began to faintly sing our country's national anthem. This only served to anger us all further as we all chanted, "Kill them, feed them to the dogs, let them rot!" We screamed out, demanding justice and blood for their wrongdoings.

"Fear not, my loyal citizens, for a sentence has been decided for them. To the older man who decided to spit, you shall be executed via firing squad by our most respected soldiers."

I and the rest of the spectators roared out cheers at this sentencing as we knew that our heroes of the war would get honored by being chosen to execute him.

"The next sentence applies to the following three prisoners. Our dogs are hungry and have had a craving for worthless slop for a while now, so you three shall be fed to the dogs."

Our cheers erupted yet again as it was a sentence that fit those who would seek to bring down our empire.

The four of them were hauled away to be held until their sentences could be carried out, leaving the crying fifth man alone on the stage.

"For the last one standing there, I leave you to the mercy of the people that you sought to kill and destroy with your horrendous acts!"

Suddenly, the bars that separated us from the stage sunk into the floor. We took this as our chance to carry out his sentence, swarming him and bumbling him with fists and feet as he begged us to stop. We enjoyed his begging. It fueled us to destroy him more as we enacted bloody vengeance upon the so-called man who sought to destroy all of us.

We felt his bones shatter, his blood splatter across our bodies and his lungs collapse against the weight of our feet. Even after he was long dead we continued until he was nothing more than a heap of crushed organs and crimson blood. We then backed away from him, leaving the body for the members of the clean-up department to clean whatever remained of his body before we went about our lives. The Execution of the rest of the prisoners would happen the next day. This way the fear inside of them could fester and boil for a day, letting the fear and dread creep through their brains until it feels like their veins flow with the essence of hopelessness rather than blood.

With my work done and the executions decided I headed home. I walked down the streets of the city, which were mostly empty because most of the citizens were still at their jobs. Due to my many years of service to the country, I was rewarded with my current job which allows me to please our leaders and I don't have to work for very long.

As I walked I decided to look around. The tall buildings of the city pierced the sky, showing off the industrial might of the country. As I walked, my gaze met a small box that was sitting in a dark alleyway. I would've missed it if I hadn't happened to look directly at it. It was red and the outside casing seemed to be made out of a very soft fabric. I don't know why I picked it up. It was as if some unseen force had compelled me to do so. I took it home and began to examine it, wondering what exactly it could be. I turned it upside down and saw a small cr ank.

I curiously began to turn the crank, but nothing happened and eventually, the crank seemed to get stuck. Slightly disappointed, I let go of the crank, but the box started to make a noise, causing me to get startled and throw the box into the wall. It hit the floor. I backed away as the noise continued, not sure what it was doing or what was going to happen next. It was a slow, somewhat high-pitched sound that had a clear rhythm to it. I slowly moved closer to the box, grabbed a pole, and poked it from a distance.

It didn't seem dangerous and the noise that it played seemed to give me a strange feeling of calmness as if someone had just removed a heavy weight from my shoulders. After about a minute of the noise it slowly fell silent once again. I had a strange compulsion to have the noise come back so I quickly ran over and began to turn the crank again. The rhythmic noise played once again, and a sense of joy seemed to flood inside of me as if it was a happy memory from long ago.

I continued this process until I passed out from exhaustion but I awoke with so much energy. It was as if I had received extra strength, I felt like I could do anything like I was overflowing with joy. I looked over at the small red box and couldn't help but smile. I grabbed it, put it under my shirt, and headed off to work.

The walk felt different today, less meaningful. I have a hard time explaining it but it just overall felt less like the glorious walk I always had, and slightly more dead. The buildings lost a bit of meaning, the sky seemed greyer, and I felt less excited about having to do my job. I quickly dashed these thoughts as I considered them impossible and chalked it up to not getting enough sleep last night. I felt the box press against me under my shirt, and it helped calm me. On my way to work, I noticed more members of the education department putting up memorials and posters on the buildings that were destroyed yesterday. There were three destroyed buildings, just like they said at the execution. I could have sworn I only saw one yesterday.

I eventually arrive at my station with a sigh as I flipped the switch that showed that I was ready to start. Before any requests came in, I had a moment to recall the sounds of the box. Remembering its sweet sounds put me in almost a dream-like trance before I was startled back to reality by the dinging sound of a request. I had gotten the same amount of orders that day as the last, which made sense, today was the execution of the rest of the criminals. The screen would light up with a small beep and would say either white, brown, or pink. It was in the same order as it was in every execution. I usually didn't mind this, but today I felt the sluggishness and the repetitiveness of it. The day seemed to drag on and on, and my glorious position suddenly seemed less glorious. I had this strange urge to just go home and listen to that box again regardless of this special event. At that moment, the glory of witnessing the day's execution paled in comparison to the joy of listening to those wonderful sounds.

The usual number of orders came and went. When I had finished, I pushed the chair out so I could stand up and went to flip the switch down to show I was finished. As my fingers touched the switch, however, I saw that the screen had lit up again with a 'beep.' Not only did having one extra order confuse me but what the screen itself said baffled me. It said, "white and brown," Something like this had never happened before. I didn't even know it could happen. I thought it was a mistake at first, but as I kept looking at the screen, that's what it read, "white and brown." I quickly sat back down in my chair, nearly falling over in the process before getting to work on the order.

I took great care with this one, even more so than I usually would. I made sure the amount was just right, going no more than three inches above the cup. I also made sure that there was a perfect balance between the white and brown flavors so that one flavor would not overtake the other. I even made sure that the swirls on top were perfect. It wasn't in the rules, it had to be so, but for some reason, I had a strong compulsion to make this order as perfect as it possibly could be. As I finished, I gently pushed it out the small window to whoever had ordered it. I stood up from my chair before I heard a small voice come from the other side of the wall that simply said, "Thank you."

I had never heard those words before, I wasn't entirely sure what they had met but they gave a sort of gratification in my work that I had never really felt before. The words were said in such a calm way, with no malice or hidden agenda behind them. They were just genuine, honest words as if they came from the leader himself. I tried to come up with something to say but I did not know how to respond. I simply nodded even though I knew full well that they couldn't see my response. It was the best I could do. I pushed my chair in and walked out of the sealed workplace and back into the street, on my way to witness the next execution.

The execution by way of the dogs was about to take place and a crowd had already begun to grow. I quickly added myself to the crowd, shoving my way to the front to get the best view. A glass room had been set up in the center of town and the three who were placed inside of it were the formally emotionless twin girls and a man. However, they were no longer emotionless and oblivious. They were full of fear. Their eyes looked as though they had stared into endless oblivion and they shook as if they had been thrown into a tundra that had turned their blood to ice. It appeared that the reality of their situation had finally gotten to them, and they finally realized their lives were at an end.

"My citizens, the great sons, and daughters of our empire." The speakers boomed with the voice of our leader, "These three sought to destroy us and killed so many of us in bombings. They seek to destroy us, they seek to destroy everything we have in this great nation we have built. We shall show these sacks of flesh a bloody vengeance that shall echo throughout the entire empire to discourage anyone from terrorizing us again!" The voice yelled so loud the microphone sounded like it would break. We all cheered and screamed in approval for what our leader was saying. He was our voice, our wills made manifest, and he was the one who will lead us to victory.

Soldiers came out of nearby buildings with heavy metallic armor that covered their chests, gloves that were strong enough to punch steel and not hurt their hands, and some sort of thick plating on the legs and boots. They were members of the juggernaut guard. This was shown not only by their heavy armor but also in their headwear. It was a completely black helmet that covered the whole head, with black glass that was where the face was. There were two blue orbs of light where a normal person's eyes would be, the color blue being the color of the juggernaut guard. You couldn't make out any features of their face. Any normal human wouldn't be able to move in so much armor, however, they moved as if they weighed nothing at all. The only way I knew they were human was because they had two arms, two legs, and a head on top of their shoulders.

The two of them held long metal poles, at the end of which were the two dogs. They were hellish creatures whose skin looked stretched as if it was taken from something else, their eyes glowed a reddish-orange as if their eyes were made from flames. They had huge muscles that pushed up their skin, however, they looked implanted. The muscles were disproportionate, too big in some places and too small in others. They snarled and drooled a mix of saliva and blood as they tried to tug away from the long poles, desperately wanting to feast upon the flesh of the prisoners inside the glass.

Even with their immense strength, the soldiers struggled to hold back the dogs. Even though no sounds of struggle came from them, I could tell by how hard they struggled that they were hardly able to keep them at bay. The three prisoners let out screams and cry as they cowered in the furthest corner of the room away from the entrance. But this wouldn't save them. As soon as they opened the door they let the monsters off their poles. They were on them in less than a second, their huge frames easily bringing them down as their teeth and claws tore away their flesh. They devoured the twins first, ripping their limbs from their bodies and the skin and muscles from their bones. Their screams didn't even get a chance to finish before the life in their eyes vanished and they once again became emotionless husks

.

The dogs slowly moved to the man, eyeing him, moving around him as a moth moves around a flame. They were entranced by him, studying him, making him slowly overcome with fear. I saw the man's mind break from stress. His brain had completely checked out before the dogs finally tore him apart. I still cheered, and I was still glad that life had left his body, but I felt strange about it. It wasn't as fulfilling. It felt like it wasn't supposed to happen. His behavior and the look the man had in his eyes before he died didn't look like those of a terrorist. They didn't look like the eyes of a man who would seek to destroy everything that we've made

.

I tried to stop these thoughts, as showing any kind of sympathy towards those who would do something like this was the worst kind of crime. But when I saw the bloodied remains of the accused, which were now nothing more than clumps of meat in front of me, I couldn't help but see them as people. I couldn't handle this, I started to feel hot, and uncomfortable as if my world was closing in around me. I pushed my way through the crowd but it felt like trying to move lead. Everything felt so heavy and my legs felt as though they were going to collapse at any moment.

My vision got darker and darker and all the noise around me sounded as though it was coming from inside my head. The crowd seemed to stretch on and on for an eternity, a never-ending swarm of buzzing noise and never-ending darkness.

I was eventually able to claw myself free of the crowd and I took a deep breath of fresh air. My vision came back to me, and the buzzing left my head, however, my heart felt like it was trying to pound out of my chest. I began to head home as quickly as I could, heaving air with nearly every step of the way as my lungs desperately breathed in so my body wouldn't collapse to the floor beneath me. I saw the building I lived in and it had never looked so beautiful in my entire life. I threw open the door to the building and dragged my body up the stairs to my room before slamming the door shut and collapsing on my floor.

As I slumped onto the floor, I felt something in my shirt press against my chest. I dug inside my shirt and realized that it was the music box, I had completely forgotten about it. I took it out and quickly began to turn the crack as much as I could. The noise filled the air once again. I began to feel better, the soft, soothing noise bringing me a small state of calm and even a bit of joy. I felt lighter as I laid back on my bed, feeling as though if I tried hard enough I would simply float away. Part of me wanted that, to simply float away and leave this whole place, this room, this city, possibly even the whole empire, and just float away into the sky where I could hear this melody forever.

However, I didn't bother trying to dash these thoughts. They calmed me and I felt too at peace to even think of trying to stop the state of euphoria that I was in. It was peaceful and calming, but I considered it strange that I had never felt this before. Our empire was so great and perfect yet I had never felt such a pure sense of happiness before. Shouldn't this be how I always felt? Why did this tiny box of sounds bring me such a feeling when living in my grand empire did not? In fact, after hearing the noises of the box it seemed to make living here worse as I felt less satisfaction in not just my work, but also in my everyday life.

The skies seemed greyer, the buildings seemed less grand, and the people seemed less like people. Everyone seemed like nothing more than ants, going about their duties because they were bred to do so with no actual life behind their cold eyes. Why was I just realizing that we have no true lives outside of our own? I was torn in two mentally, I didn't know where these thoughts came from and I hated having them. For twenty years I have been told and shown that we have no flaws and that we are the greatest nation under the sun. For twenty years I saw evidence of this but why did that evidence seem so contradictory to me when it had not before?

I came to realize I was being irrational. Twenty years of proof shouldn't be questioned by some noise. The small box stopped making its noise and I did not turn the crank for the rest of that night. I lay in my bed and slowly drifted off to sleep, letting the peaceful dark slowly come over me and take me somewhere far away.

Months passed by and my delusions slowly subsided because I had stopped listening to the small box of noise. My job had been going well and I always looked forward to the special mixed order I got at the end. I always enjoyed the "thank you". I still didn't know what it meant, but it still gave me the level of pride that it always did. On the last day I worked there I even got to see the man's eyes and a small part of his face. Those crystal blue eyes stared right into mine as he once again simply said, "Thank you." I was astonished by this because this was banned. Why someone who was one of the people in charge of running the empire would do this baffled me, but I paid it no major mind.

The next day, I received a letter saying that I would be given a new job in a personnel organization. I would look at a citizen's file (the empire had files on every citizen) and if they had any violations I would stamp it with an X and they would receive appropriate punishment. If they had no violations, I'd stamp it with an O. With the job also came a new uniform, a black jacket with a white button-up undershirt and black tie.

I arrived excited on the first day. There was a single guard who stood at the door to make sure no one except for me entered. I went into the room. It was lavish and wonderfully decorated. The chair and desk were long cold metal, but with a cushioned seat with armrests. The table was that of high-quality wood. I quickly got to work, going through the large stack of papers in front of me and marking them with either Xs or Os. I had a sense of pride with each stamp, knowing that it made the empire a better place. The job went quickly that day as I was so sucked in. The man from outside came into the room, "Time's up," he said as he held open the door for me. I nodded, stood up, and headed home. I felt a large amount of pride that day, but the pride would not last long.

The next day, I arrived again to do the job, eager to continue my work. I did the same thing that day, marking profiles with Xs and Os. All was normal until one file. I saw the face of the citizen on the paper. It was a small child, a little boy, no older than ten years old. I looked over the heights and weights to see if the picture was some kind of mistake but no he had the average height and weight for a child.

I walked up to the man outside the room and said, "Sir, I think there has been a mistake on this file."

He took the file and looked it over "What mistake?" I was slightly surprised by his response, "Sir, he's a child."

"Children can be just as dangerous as adults when following extremists. Bombs placed by a child, do the same amount of damage as bombs placed by an adult." He shoved the file back into my hands. "Now don't question the empire's reasoning again."

"My apologies sir," I stepped back into the room and grabbed the X stamp because the file said that the boy was suspected of terrorism, treason, and stealing supplies. After looking into the boy's smiling face for what seemed like an eternity, I stamped the file with an X.

This work kept going on for months. There were more children that I would have to stamp with an X, but it never became easy. The stamp always seemed to be so much heavier whenever I saw a child's face, some being as young as six years old. But, it was the right thing to do right because these kids were terrorists, killers, and thieves. Why should I feel guilty?

I listened to the announcements by our leader every day, did my work, attended executions, and still felt pride in my country and work. I lived in this perception of reality for months, ignoring everything that was lying just underneath the surface of my perception. Until that one night that is. That night I made a decision that changed everything. I listened to the box again.

I arrived one last night after a draining day of work. Fifteen files I had gone through that day belonged to children, and all were stamped with an X. I collapsed on my bed, heavy and tired as if my bones were made of lead. I turned my head to the side, facing the small counter on the side of my bed. On top of the counter, it sat, the small red box. I never realized it was sitting there before. Had that been where I set it all those months ago, I thought I had lost it. Did I just forget, or did I just somehow not see it?

I shook my head to dash these questions because they weren't important. What was important was the fact that I was exhausted. Even though the memory of the box had begun to fade, I remember the feeling it gave, one of joy and weightlessness. I began to turn the crank that was settled in the bottom of the box until it was tight and wouldn't crank anymore. Before I released my grip I hesitated because I remembered the sort of thoughts I had while listening to the box, thoughts that would make me stamp my file with an X should anyone else hear them. But, I needed this. The weight I was carrying was too much and I needed to be weightless again.

I let go of the handle and I began to feel everything become like silk. I felt as if I was cutting through the air itself, weightless, careless, and even somewhat lifeless. I laid flat on my bed in a state of pure relief because I thought this is what freedom feels like, my first of many treasonous thoughts of the night. I hardly cared anymore. However, the feeling was too wonderful to have any sense of doubt. I listened to that box for hours and hours. It brought endless joy that night. I feared it would bring upon me a horrible realization the next day.

I woke up the next day with a smile on my face and in a wonderful mood. As I got dressed though I remembered what I'd have to do at work that day and my smile quickly faded. I looked at the box and decided to take it with me to work in hopes that it would brighten my mood. I packed it into my shirt and left, quickly walking to work because I didn't want to observe the drab world that was around me, but I saw glances of a world coming apart at the seams. Buildings that should have been destroyed, buildings that should have still stood tall. How was I only seeing this now? I shook my head, it had to be my imagination, how could there be lies, it was the box like it always was.

I arrived at work, sweat dripping down my face, and quickly walked into the room. I moved through the stack of papers in front of me, simply trying to focus on my work and what good service I was doing to our empire. But then another seam came undone my world when one of the files turned my blood cold. I saw a man with a pair of crystal blue eyes staring up at me from that piece of paper. I shivered as I realized I had seen those eyes before. They were the same eyes that always ordered mixed flavors, the man who had always said thank you, the man who dared to look at a servus.

His file said that he was accused of speaking with the servus and even directly gazing at one, something they were never allowed to do. I felt guilt, I felt responsible for this man. After all, he was only here because he chose to speak to me.

"No, why would he speak to me, I am nothing special, just a servus like everyone else, why should I feel blamed?" I thought to myself, but this was a lie, a vain attempt to block out guilt and shame, a way of deflecting to try and solve the war raging on in my head. I have no idea how long I sat there. It felt like only seconds had gone by, yet it somehow also felt like I had been sitting there for years. I gritted my teeth so hard that they felt like they could shatter at any moment, but knowing the possible ramifications I stamped his file with an O.

I stood to leave, taking a look at the man who was guarding the door. He gave me a look back that radiated an emptiness that felt like if I looked at him for too long I would be sucked into a neverending void. I quickly looked away and left that building as quickly as I could. I needed some kind of peace of mind, I needed some kind of voice to say that I was doing the right thing, that the world I knew was crumbling apart and shattering all around me. I needed to know that everything that I knew wasn't a lie that had been spoon-fed to me for the entirety of my life. I rushed to the center of town to hear the daily speech from the leader.

I stood with the rest of the crowd, waiting to hear his words. Surely his words would install patriotism back into me, and show me that I was just being paranoid. Surely that would be the case. This was all something in my head brought upon by stress, or that box.

"That's it. It's the box," I said quietly to myself. I reached inside my coat jacket, and was about to take it out, and smash it on the ground, but then the microphone spoke, and I was sent into a mental spiral.

The voice that came out of the microphone, the voice of our leader, was different. It sounded younger, a bit less experienced, and less commanding. I didn't hear what the voice said, I couldn't hear anything anymore. My brain was trying to understand what was happening. I looked around and everyone else reacted as if the voice had always sounded like this. How could they not realize that the voice we heard all our lives was now different, it was different right?

Before I knew it I was running, running as fast and as far as I could. This was all wrong, it was all wrong. Flashes of everything I'd done went through my mind, watching public executions and cheering, seeing people get torn apart and laughing, beating a person to death, and smiling. The begging, the crying, pleading, it all only made me smile wider. What was I? Was I a servus, something less, something more, a human, a monster, an undesirable? It was too much, I couldn't handle it and I eventually collapsed and passed out in the middle of the street.

When I awoke I was in an underground tunnel, surrounded by others. One of them spoke, "He's awake, good." I looked around and saw dozens of boxes like my own, all in different colors,

"Where am I?" I asked groggily. My head was pounding hard. "You'll learn in time," a man said and helped me up. All the others in the cave looked over me as if they were studying me. "Welcome to the real world, sir."

These people were like me. They had all found boxes that played those noises, I always thought our anthem was the only thing like that. I learned everything. They had bombed us to further the narrative that we were under attack, and more tragedy furthers their message. Innocent people were executed as well. If they made it seem like there was a large enemy to fight then it would cause more fear so they could tighten their grip further. Using fear, and changing our language to exclude certain words is a grander tool to manipulate us. Making us think there is an enemy, that there are people somehow less than us, that they are strong in being a threat to us, but also weak because they stood no chance. They idolize war and war heroes rather than focusing on peace furthering us.

It stops now. We will make a difference. It won't be a swift change but it starts now. We will be the change, the light in the dark. We will bring the empire to a new peace and make something better.

This is our history. The world our ancestors lived in must never happen again, or all their struggles will have been for nothing.

Made in the USA
Middletown, DE
28 October 2024

62948577R00071